A WEIRD FICTION TALE III:
THE FOOL'S JOURNEY

A Weird Fiction Tale III: The Fool's Journey

Copyright © 2024 by JCC Chavez, Jr.

Cover Artwork by Mestizo Ink Productions

Cover Design and Interior Formatting by Melissa Williams Design

ISBN (print): 978-1-7360633-5-4

ISBN (eBook): 978-1-7360633-6-1

A WEIRD FICTION TALE III:
THE FOOL'S JOURNEY

• • • •

JCC CHAVEZ, JR.

CHAPTER 1
SINS OF THE FATHER

January 21, 2229, in the present.

"How long has it been . . . since your brother's passing?" Bloodstone asks, eyes gleaming with compassion. His righthand twitches, yearning to reach her cold, distant one. He recognizes the plaintive cry that has kept her silent and isolated from everyone, including him. Winter has come, and amid its winds sweeps the memory of Miss Sierra's deceased brother, Santiago.

"Not long enough." Miss Sierra finally replies with a shaky voice.

The Immortal Luchador smiles at her. He is happy to see her aware of the noble intentions behind his reserved question.

Miss Sierra doesn't return his smile. Instead, her eyes quiver with a thin veil of tears. She continues, "No matter the years that may've passed, the memory of it follows me everywhere I go. I've tried to keep it asleep. A stupid notion, I know." She wraps herself in her arms, and she shivers. Though Bloodstone knows it's not from the cold air. "It's like a shadow. Whenever I wake up, it's right there on the ground, tickling my toes. It's hard to ignore it when it grows bigger and stronger with the sun setting. Seven years . . . for seven years, I've been drowning in these shadows. I've lived in the blanket of night for that long, Mister Bloodstone, and without the comfort of any glinting stars."

"But words can offer you comfort, Miss Sierra," Bloodstone sighs. He swerves a broad, muscular arm around his back and begins to rub off the pain with a raking hand. He hunches over, eager, and willing to help carry the weight of her sorrow. "Words offer us a means to exorcise our pains and mend our wounds. Though scars will endure, it is a better alternative to what shadows offer us—enslavement eternal to our grief."

"I appreciate your kindness Mister Bloodstone." Miss Sierra's left cheek pulls to the side, and her grief-filled eyes glimpse his tender gaze before shying away to the snow-pelted night. "But I'm not quite ready to share my grief with you just yet. Friendly as we may be, we're still no more than strangers. Please, don't be offended by this."

"Worry not, my dear. My heart remains unharmed. I more than understand." Bloodstone replies coolly, though he has no intention to waver. Over a month ago, Miss Sierra staked her own life to help him retrieve his stolen treasure, a childhood gift from his beloved Mamá Sofía. She did more than enough to prove herself a true friend, and now, he intends to honor that very friendship. "But, perhaps, you can find the strength to share some details of the tragedy with me. Just enough to sate my stubborn heart."

"There was snow, soft as silk. Its ivory calmness was a cruel lie meant to blind us to the curse that threatened us," Miss Sierra recalls with a steady voice. "And then there was the band of lost souls. They arrived at our quaint little town by the mountains, sacrificial lambs tasked with purging the great evil that ailed our lands. There were three of them, bounty killers. Two were heartless bastards, men true to their profession. Men cursed with an insatiable hunger for avarice."

"And what of the third?" Bloodstone asks. "What curse bedeviled him?"

"The worst sort of curse. The sort of curse that compels you to take up the burdensome choices and sins of cowards and fools." She replies, spellbound by the outside falling snow. "He was different . . . he . . . he was a hero."

September 8, 2221, sometime in the past.

A solitary man pierces through the briny mist. A rucksack teeters on his back. It is fat with a small tent, excavating tools, maps, a journal, and pencils, and a single waterskin swings from the left shoulder strap. He wheezes with a hot breath, for he is a willowy man of fair skin and fine, soft red hair that curls all round his crinkly face.

He continues to stride through the thinning mist with the shaky legs of a green frontiersman.

The night before, an earthquake swiped across the mountainous town of Berumbo. It was a seismic roar of a damnable fury that could've cleaved the surrounding mountains. The townsfolk fluttered and cooed about like addled, rattled quails. Snowstorms are the natural pitfalls which terrorize the people of

Berumbo, but never tremors. Though their superstitions were stirred awake, most of the townsfolk retreated to the quiet comforts of mundane life.

But Salvatore Antonio Sierra is above these simple campesinos. He is a lettered man. He is a desperate man, cursed with a bottomless hunger to restore his lost honor. He is eager to seek out penance for his sins through the act of discovery.

Salvatore's outmoded seismometer readings have led him beyond the town's boundary, through the mountains, down their northwestern slopes to where the town cemetery lay, and finally into the western coastline. The migration was wretched, a dangerous undertaking pledged long before the dawn cracked through the darkness of night. Jaguars are the infallible hunters in these mysterious ridges, and Salvatore is a lone, nude trespasser upon their realm. He'd be utterly endangered to the jaguars' remorseless claws and fangs if not for the hunting rifle clasped with quivering hands. Salvatore is afraid of encountering one of these fair hunters even after breaching the mountains. Yet, he continues to wander, dauntless, down the coastline and towards the cove, towards the epicenter of the supernatural anomaly.

His knees buckle and a vertigo spin pulls him down toward the moist sand. The breakers thin to a gentle streak between his fingers. Salvatore leans against the hunting rifle, takes in a deep breath, and then uses it like a shepherd's staff to hoist himself up.

As he stands, a low growl waylays his trudge. Two golden eyes glister behind the melting mist, and the jaguar creeps out. Its appearance laves Salvatore with fear, and he is unable to lift the rifle's overweight barrel. But the jaguar's merciful purr quashes his fears.

The jaguar swivels its glance between Salvatore and the cove. It growls at him and walks away, back to its kingdom in the mountains. Salvatore sighs sharply and is in utter disbelief; the jaguar's fear was visible and eclipsed his own. And its growl warned at an unknown darkness that lay beyond the reach of unimaginative eyes. A darkness mightier than the jaguar and lying just ahead in the cove, but Salvatore espouses ambition above the jaguar's portend fear.

He scratches his curly, red beard with discomfort, and continues down the coastline.

Salvatore then makes a serendipitous discovery—a cave has sprung to life in the cove. Berumbo and its mountains are Salvatore's true mothers, and he knows every surrounding fissure and ridge and coastline like his own body. This cave has never existed before today, the day of its mysterious birth. He tiptoes closer toward the newborn cave's mouth. A ghostly breeze howls back to him, but Salvatore shuns reasonable instinct, lights a lantern, and invades the unknown coldness. He reaches a large open chamber and chases the darkness away with the lantern to study the surrounding cavity.

He discovers skull glyphs chiseled on the rock, and the rock is cut and stacked into tunnels that burrow deeper into the cave with sculptures of giant shark monsters guarding the entrances. Salvatore has discovered something wondrous. This cave is no natural occurrence. It is a structure of an intelligent design.

"The glory of such a marvelous discovery will be mine alone. I acted quickly and sought the support of my closest childhood friend, Osvaldo 'Oz' Amadeo Barrio." Salvatore narrates the same thoughts he pens over his journal. "Osvaldo gathered us a team of twenty strong countrymen, four mules, two carriages stocked full of camping supplies and archeological supplies, plus two female oxen. Berumbo is a small town, isolated from the greater world, almost a mere ghost to outsiders, a fact that is beneficial to my wish of keeping the cave's site and miraculous birth a secret from outsiders. This glory will be mine—it must be mine."

He continues, "Against my wife Charlotte's protests, I resolved to taking both our children along with me on the dig. Both Rubí and our youngest and lone son, Santiago, are eager to join their father. It is a great new adventure set forth by the anthem of innocence. An anthem belying to the horrors that might await us buried underneath the cave's nebulous origin."

The first day goes about without incident. Base camp is set at the first chamber's epicenter, just a few meters away from the cave entrance. Tents are erected, lights juiced with power generators, and the excavation is underway within hours.

"Just when we thought that the world was barren of miracles and wonders." Salvatore comments aloud. He and Osvaldo bury their hands deep into the virgin soil like giddy children, careless of their stiff backs, buckled knees and swollen muscles. They continue grinding the soil well into the late hours of the night.

By the second day, with a few winks of rest between digs, both men have recorded dozens of arcane religious artifacts, the bulk made up of several ivory masks. The dig continues deeper into the cave while Salvatore logs reams of the glyphs in detailed notes. Yet, the ivory masks catch his uttermost interest above all things.

Salvatore recognizes the familiar, dead symbol engraved above the brow area of each mask—a hollow eye pierced with eight arrows, their spears jutting away from the mask's wearer with an unmistakable threat.

Salvatore runs a single finger over one of the masks' groves. He blinks, its presence among the artifacts shakes him to the bone.

"Whatever were you doing here?" Salvatore mouths to himself and sketches the design in his journal before tossing it to the side with revulsion. He turns to Osvaldo. "Gather up all of these masks and have them destroyed on the fires."

"What? What did you just say?" Osvaldo's brows twist with puzzlement. "Don't you think that'll be a careless thing to do, Sal? We came here as explorers and you're asking me to do something that's even beneath graverobbers."

"I spoke clearly so as to avoid repetition, Oz." Salvatore argues and attempts to march away. "Have them destroyed, burn every last one."

"Hey, not before you explain yourself, *compadre*." Osvaldo hooks Salvatore's left arm. He studies him with suspicious eyes. He then lets off a wry chuckle. "You sly bastard. You've seen these masks and their markings before. What do you know about them?"

"Enough, I know enough." Salvatore replies with a hoarse tone. He wriggles his arm free from Osvaldo's grasp. "I've scoured the world long enough and seen enough to understand that these masks must be burned. No valuable knowledge will be lost with their ashes."

Osvaldo clicks his tongue. Salvatore recognizes that irritable tic of his. "You're sounding like a superstitious fool. What exactly are you trying to ward off here?"

"Misfortune and misery," Salvatore answers and walks away.

Salvatore then follows his men deeper into the cave. They snail down a ravine until they reach an enclosed pond with more tunneled pathways. Salvatore is now convinced; This is no cave, but a buried structure that erupted out of the rock—a tower! They found nothing more of value in the lower chamber except for another mask of basalt stone. Salvatore considers the mask's banality with little regard. Unlike the ivory masks, the stone mask's grain is native to the tower. Still, it is unremarkable and of no visible value. So, he hands it to his children when they return to camp. Boredom has since dulled Rubí and Santiago's earlier enthusiasm. Salvatore hopes the trifling mask will provide them with some entertainment while he focuses on the rest of the excavation.

"Sonny, that's not funny!" Rubí yells.

Santiago chases her around, barking and growling like a monster with the mask paste over his face.

"Stop it, Sonny! I'm not laughing. Just take that ugly thing off already." Rubí chides.

"Sure sissy. Just take yours off first. Oh wait, that's just your face." Santiago teases.

Salvatore chuckles at their childish bickering.

"The fatherly thing for me to do is to break off Santiago's bullying. Then again, Rubí and Santiago can rarely be children. With their stern mother away, I consider it appropriate to allow them to torment one another like normal, happy siblings. Perhaps this is the fatherliest thing I can do for them right now."

He escapes back to his notes, ashamed of the amusement their harmless spat gives him.

The sun sinks onto the swerving ocean waves and gives way to the stars and moon, marking the end of the second day's hard work.

Midway through his notes, a sudden jolt over his right shoulder halts Salvatore's scribing. He looks up, and to his sincere surprise, Osvaldo scowls down at him. Osvaldo nudges his head toward Salvatore's children. Both are slumped near a small bonfire, appearing miserable and lonesome.

"Sal, you've been doodling for hours. I think it's best you stop right now before your hand cramps up into a claw." Osvaldo said with a stern glare. He is an observant old codger and godfather to Rubí and Santiago. He and his wife, Paciencia, take pride in their anointed roles, and see both children as the ones they've been denied. "Take a break *compadre*. We'll be here for two weeks straight, and, um, considering the way things are going between you and that bitch, who knows if you'll ever savor another peaceful night with them."

"I don't appreciate the crude remark, Oz. Things between me and Charlotte are ugly at best, but she's still my wife and you'll show her proper respect." Salvatore knows it's futile to try to ignore the problems in his marriage to Charlotte. But he has lacked quality time with his children throughout the expedition. He meets Osvaldo with a downcast look. "I'd love to spend time with them. But, Oz, you know just as well as I, that this is the find of the century. We need this—*I* need this."

"Sad truth is *compadre*; nothing you do today or tomorrow will ever change the past. Time's trajectory is always forward." Osvaldo lectures Salvatore. He nibbles at the dirt wedged between his fingernails and spits it out. "And the way I see it, Sal, the things we've dug up here today are quite comfortable being ignored and forgotten. That don't mean we got to treat our true treasures the same way."

Salvatore gives off a heavy sigh. Osvaldo speaks a hard truth—Rubí and Santiago are his true salvation. He clips the pen, shuts the journal, and rises to his feet.

"I'm resigning myself from the dig for the

rest of the night. I'm leaving the remainder of the glyphic transcription to you." Salvatore says to Osvaldo and maneuvers his way around the other working hands and dust clouds to join his neglected children. On his way, Salvatore pulls out a wooden shape from his jacket's left pocket. He'd been whittling at it for days, and he quickly carves out the final smaller details of the miniature wooden jaguar for Rubí. His children's longing frowns spring to broad smiles the moment he joins them by the fire.

For the past seven years, Salvatore's marriage to Charlotte has been teetering on the fringes of disillusionment, and twelve years have passed since his noble intentions blackened his honor.

Rubí and Santiago may've inherited his surname, but Rubí is a daughter to him alone. Charlotte bestows the daughter title to her out of sheer vanity and pride—to preserve the secret of her humiliation. Salvatore betrayed their great love, and his betrayal blessed an innocent with a mother's contempt.

Charlotte's first pregnancy was a dark fairy-tale. Rubí is not the child they were promised. Their first child was stillborn, a deformed, tiny cadaver laved deep in red with its mother's blood.

The delivery cost Charlotte much blood, and she was left unconscious when it finally passed. The midwife then presented Salvatore with their dead newborn. Salvatore swore the midwife to secrecy, hoping to spare Charlotte from an uncurable grief. He then swaddled the dead infant in a black cloth, braved the harsh winter winds, and buried it in the dirt and snow somewhere atop the highest and farthest mountain peak—away from Berumbo and away from its mother's yearning touch. There, the unborn infant will remain dead, buried, and forgotten.

The blood of the dead birth seeped through the cloth. Salvatore's hands were wet with the ugliness of his lovesick sin. He wept and hammered the frozen earth with clenched fists. The fires of sorrow shielded him from the cold howl, even when his tears froze around his cheeks. Then, a tiny wail lured Salvatore away from his forsaken child's snowy tomb. A little, newborn girl cried out for a parent's love. The infant was bare and alone in the icy wasteland.

Could she have been left behind to die? A child from God, meant to supplant his loss? He did not know. Salvatore cradled the mewling infant in his two hands, and she was warm as a summer's day. He considered the child in his arms. His grief clouded his judgment, and it was his noble intentions that ultimately killed their love. The abandoned child was baptized Rubí Aquila Sierra, and she usurped the birthright of the child that never was.

For five years, Charlotte believed Rubí to be their trueborn daughter. And it was the birth of their second child, Santiago, that aroused Charlotte's suspicions over her daughter's missing birthmark. Salvatore finally confessed his sin of love, the sin that aroused Charlotte's vicious vendetta against him.

But despite everything, Salvatore's love mirrored Charlotte's unforgiving hatred. Though they continue to share the warmth of their bed, never again will they share the warmth of their bodies. Even during the hottest of summers, nights always draw cold for Salvatore.

Their love has been dead for seven years, but such a death has no bearing on his undying devotion for Rubí and Santiago. Osvaldo's brazen advice was true. There is no absolution to be found with Charlotte. His children are all that matter now, and they need reassurance of his love. Rubí more so than Santiago. While Santiago is a true testament to their extinct love, the heir to Charlotte's legacy, Rubí is the usurper, Charlotte's humiliation and Salvatore's betrayal incarnate.

"How old is this place, papa?" Rubí asks, leafing through Salvatore's journal.

Though not of his blood, Rubí embodies Salvatore's best qualities. She is studious, insightful, and honorable like him. But, in some ways, she is prideful and willful like Charlotte.

"We're not too sure yet my little moon flower." Salvatore said. He cradles a sleeping Santiago in his arms; the boy still clenches to the basalt stone mask. He carries off his weary baby boy to the tent and tucks him in inside his sleeping bag before continuing. "But it's very old. Perhaps even untold millennia. We know so little still, except that it sprung out of the earth like magick."

"That's silly." Rubí replied.

"Oh, and why is that moon flower?" Salvatore asks with that warm, rare smile of his. He nods, encouraging her to continue.

"There's no such thing as magick." Rubí replies, twiddling her fingers. "There is only one magick, and that's our imaginations. It can help us find stuff or get us more lost."

"Very good. I'm surprised you actually paid

attention to my lectures at the library." Salvatore laughs and takes back the journal. He then hugs her and kisses her forehead. "We've learned one thing so far, my little darling. This world is still fertile with strange miracles. Who knows what other miracles we might unearth here? But not today. The hour is late, moon flower. We should follow your brother's example and let our dreams take charge of our thinking for now." He hands the journal back to her. "Here, a little light reading before bed. Read it before morning, and you and Sonny can join me in tomorrow's dig. Would you like that?"

Rubí nods with a shy grin.

Salvatore's dreams are plagued by a great white waste.

He stands alone atop the tallest, farthest mountain from Berumbo, before a gaping hole over the snowy earth. He knows this place. It is the gravesite of his stillborn child.

"It's all just a dream," Salvatore whispers to himself. But the frost that claws his face is enough for him to question his sanity. He inspects the grave, and a wraithlike chill claws up his throat when he notices the ruptured earth. Something burst out from underneath, and it left a thin, pink trail of blood on the snow. Salvatore follows the trail around and behind him.

He turns to face the child he had abandoned in the shallow grave twelve years ago. His eyes scream in horror. His prodigal son blossomed into a malformed, skinless monstrosity. Its exposed muscles and nerves sweat with blood, and its inhuman eyes gleam milky white. The creature's wails echo the ugliness of its shape. A single, blood dripping hand reaches for Salvatore.

"Why? Why did you abandon me?" The creature's rotting breath steams and scalds Salvatore's face. "Why did you abandon me, father?"

"No! Please, stay away!" Salvatore shrieks. He pratfalls onto the snow, trying to avoid the creature's sinewy touch. "You're dead—an unborn thing. You weren't even blessed with the grace of a single breath. Stay away!"

The creature shrieks with despair over its father's rejection. Then, its shriek falls into silence over the sound of crackling bone. Salvatore turns to the sound by the southeast cliff and there it stands behind a thin sheet of drizzling snow—the Shark Monster. It is a skeletal creature with ashen skin that flakes like grating stone, and molten-blooded eyes lie hidden behind thin, oily strands of seaweed hair. The Shark Monster cackles and grins at Salvatore with its needled fangs. A deep, rotting fear steals Salvatore's screams—and he wakes to Rubí's horrified screams.

He gasps with terror and jumps out of his tent. Eyes agape with disbelief, he bears witness to the carnage unfurling before him.

A raging fire eats away the tents, and the cindering stone clouds the chamber with black smoke. His men scream in a mix of death curls and fear. Atop a throne of guts and blood, the Shark Monster stands free from Salvatore's nightmares. The Shark Monster shreds the flesh off the bones of a young man with its needled fangs and it tilts its head back, letting off a sinister cackle that echoes all throughout the chamber.

Salvatore stares into the young man's vacant, dead eyes while the Shark Monster feasts upon him. The terror numbs Salvatore to all sensation—a stream of warm blood flows cold between his bare toes.

"Sal!" Osvaldo yanks Salvatore by the shoulder, breaking his trance. He has Rubí locked in his hand. He barks at Salvatore. "What are you doing?! You damn idiot. Do you want to get gutted by that thing?! Everyone, out of the cave, now! Move! Move!"

The surviving men trip over the disemboweled cadavers and entrails and slip on the spilled blood of their slain countrymen as they flee. Salvatore carries Rubí in his arms while Osvaldo lags. Rubí trembles and whispers into Salvatore's ears, but her voice goes unheard.

They reach the outer coast with little comfort. Salvatore lays Rubí on her feet and he swivels to glance back to the cave. The Shark Monster meets his trembling gaze before it melts away back into the shadows with its molten-blooded eyes and hideous needled grin.

On a mid-summer night, the first snowflakes fell over the town of Berumbo. Out of the twenty-four-man excavation party, eight escaped the slaughter. But none walked away unscathed from fear. For years on out, their cowardice will haunt the survivors. None more than Salvatore, who abandoned another son to die.

April 12, 2222

For seven months the mountains have endured a sleepless whiteout. Berumbo has become sterile and anemic. Times are confusing for the few townsfolk who have remained behind. Even jaguars, the infallible mountain hunters, have forsaken their kingdom. A dark, preternatural curse has swept over the mountains, raped the soil, and led the peoples astray from their world's secluded normalcy and into the realm of superstition.

The sleepless snow falls heavy over Salvatore's shoulders. He lets off a weary sigh, and his breath chills to frost upon touching the accursed air. Several miles out from Berumbo, there is a waystation, and a train makes a supply drop every two weeks. And it is here that Salvatore and Osvaldo wait for a different sort of supply.

Rubí is with both men. After losing Santiago, his baby boy, Salvatore refuses to let her stray far from his sight.

"I shan't lose a third child." Salvatore looks to his lone daughter, chewing over her and Berumbo's uncertain future.

Osvaldo takes out a peach from his coat

pocket. He bites down on it and allows the thin, nectary strings to flow free down over his silver beard. He savors every bite with salivating patience, unsure if he will ever get to savor such a succulent fruit again.

"How's your wife doing these days?" Osvaldo asks, breaking their mutual thirty-minute silence.

"Better. She started eating on her own again." Salvatore answers with a blank stare. He claws his curly red beard with a shaky hand. Santiago's sudden death spiraled Charlotte into a deathlike trance for the past seven months. She has since refused to see or speak to anyone and cradles herself in the comfort of her embittered grief. "And she, um, she even spoke to me, too. She uttered one sentence alone. Four words short. Better than anything I deserve, to be honest."

"Four words? Huh. It's a step in the right direction, I suppose." Osvaldo suckles on the peach's hollow heart and then flings it to the side. "What did she say to you?"

"I want a divorce." Salvatore quotes with a hollow tone. "She didn't even look me in the eye when she said it."

"Fuck. Jesus H. Christ, I don't know what to

tell you *compadre*. You shouldn't have married that bitch, Sal. The Foix clan, entire goddamn family got a reputation for being cunts. Told you before, can't take a cunt for a bride. Sooner or later, fucking cunt will swallow you whole, cock and all." Osvaldo said with palpable disdain. His anger cools when he turns to Rubí. She did not hear his crass remark. She is distracted, sifting through a book. "Does she already know?"

"She was right there with me when Charlotte spoke it," Salvatore answers rather weary with the conversation. "I don't have to worry much about her emotional take on the matter. Rubí and Charlotte haven't bonded for years either way. Not that they ever had any reason to."

"For five years, Sal, five fucking years, she coddled her like a true mother. Duped or not, Charlotte has no reason to disown that little girl." Osvaldo snarls with clenched teeth. "She is a child, Sal. A child starved of a mother's love because of no fault of her own."

"Can we not do this right now, Oz." Salvatore snaps back. His eyes hover over to his daughter. "Not in front of Rubí. She's been through enough, or have you forgotten that?"

Osvaldo shakes his head. "We have more pressing matters to attend to right now. My marital problems and bitch of a wife are the farthest things from my mind."

Times are confusing in Berumbo. This is the first time Osvaldo has ever heard Salvatore speak about his wife in such a vulgar manner. Their marriage is now over.

Off by the distance, a billowing white cloud of boiling steam circles around the trio of hillocks, the *Tres Gorditas*. The train's whistle shrieks. It is a few minutes away from arriving at the waystation.

"You sure you want to go through with this, Sal?" Osvaldo asks with concern. He coddles himself with his stubby arms, noticing the cold air for the first time. "Maybe there's another way. Maybe we're being a tad callous here. Town's halfway dead, most families have already fled to the city. We can do the same. Sometimes there's bravery in cowardice and maybe that thing won't give chase. Maybe it'll let us be and stay behind to prey on unsuspecting hitchhikers or something. There must be another way, Sal."

"You know there isn't Oz." Salvatore said. His eyes are pinned to the approaching train.

"Lord knows I wish there was. But God isn't on this Earth anymore, is He? We've killed our God and welcomed the Devil with open arms. And it makes no difference if we stay or flee. We're cowards either way. Only cowards hire the sinful to absolve their sins."

"Jesus H. Christ, Sal. You don't need to get all sanctimonious with me. Nothing wrong with fearing damnation." Osvaldo said in resignation. "Fuck, I hate it when you make sense, though. I do pray these amoral bastards we've hired don't turn out to be pigs lined for the slaughter."

The months after the massacre at the cave, while Berumbo withered to a ghost, Salvatore and Osvaldo spent many candlelit nights deciphering Osvaldo's journal notes on the glyphs. Osvaldo's notes lacked Salvatore's predisposition for accurate detail and Salvatore's own journal lay orphaned inside the cave, lost during their desperate escape. The aboriginal writings on the walls avowed little about the Shark Monster's true heritage, but their efforts clawing at the cryptic glyphs banked them crucial knowledge about the creature's nature, a desperate victory—the Shark Monster is mortal.

Then, there was the matter of the question: who among them shall brave the unknown dark and slay the unearthed forgotten?

At this crux, Osvaldo suggested they hire warriors of fortune, bounty killers, to carry out the dirty deed. He had personal ties with the Bounty Killers Guild, being on a first name base with the newly appointed Guild Master, Neza.

Osvaldo made the call, and Neza booked his best bounty killers for the job, including a special agent among the three.

"Rubí, come stand next to me," Salvatore calls to his daughter.

The three-cart train blurs past them. It comes to a trudging stop. The train's engine pants, and from the first cart, a wooden door slides open. The conductor tosses out a hefty lump, the daily mail, and it lands near their toes. Then another door slides open, this time from the third, farthest cart. A man, clad in a knee-long duster, boots with spurs, and a cowboy hat, jumps out from the cart.

The bounty killers have arrived at Berumbo.

CHAPTER 2
THE CURSED AND THE DAMNED

The train arrives at the waystation at 6:45 p.m. and one by one, the bounty killers exit.

Each is a deplorable creature. Whether they are victims of their heinous nature or cruel circumstance, it is insignificant. They are cursed men for they walk through the darkest valley of sin and death for survival's sake. Yet, these very same men have been convoked to deliver Berumbo from damnation.

Alonso Severino de Santa Ana is the first to exit the cart. He cements his boots onto the snowy wooden platform. Twin bandoliers are strapped to his shoulders, underscoring the caramel man's reputable sobriquet, the Lucky Kid. His weapons of choice are twin pistols, strapped to his thighs on holsters, and he keeps a custom made four-barrel rifle strapped to his back.

Santa Ana is a modern-day Billy the Kid, a gentleman killer whose murderous appetites are reined back. But the mask of calmness veils Santa Ana's gluttony for ultraviolence and wanton fornication. Not much of a braggart, Santa Ana is humble about the high number of his kills and sexual conquests.

Vicenzo Francesco Savani—Savani to his partners—is the next heinous bastard to jump out of the cart. A thick, frizzled porcupine beard is the sole patch of hair that provides his grotesque, balding head with some warmth. The hideous man is of a fit built. His biceps breathe free from the sleeveless duster coat and his muscular chest lays unfettered by an under-shirt. The cold scathes him none, nor does it slacken his pedophiliac appetites. His twisted, mad eyes snare young Rubí, and septic fanta-sies begin to swirl in his rotten brain.

Savani discharges a lewd drool, and he licks his piranha-like teeth. He tightens the sinewy grip around the pair of thorn-studded brass knuckles wrapped around his hands. The per-verse instruments of death are named Rosie and

Daisy after his first two victims. Both twelve-year old girls' skulls and horrified screams were ground to mulch by these very same instruments of death. Rosie and Daisy are relics of Savini's inbred curse.

Savani's hungry grope disturbs Rubí, and she scurries behind her father.

A timid child with no one to call mother or friend, Rubí, is a little bird naive about the greater world beyond her tiny nest. Though unlearned about the darkness that influences humanity, she is eager to take flight. But Salvatore's overprotective grip holds her down firm at her feet. And Santiago's death has only tightened that very grip. These bounty killers are the first foreigners she has ever witnessed visit their accursed and isolated little town. She finds them unsavory emissaries of the outside world. A view that will be challenged when the third bounty killer finally exits the cart.

"You must be Salvatore. The old man from the guild sent us," Santa Ana said, chewing tobacco between his gums. He saunters towards Salvatore. "Name's Santa Ana, leader of this here band of killers, and we're here to kill your monster."

"Yes, a pleasure to make your acquaintance.

This here is my colleague, Osvaldo." Salvatore pauses for a moment. He notices they are shy one bounty killer. "I thought we were promised three of you. Where's the third?"

Santa Ana hawks and spits out a muddy ball of saliva on Salvatore's shoes. Salvatore never addresses the disrespectful act.

"Bloody hell. Where's that bastard at?" Santa Ana storms back to the cart. He barks inside with gnashing teeth. "You're still asleep in there, kid?! Get your ass out here, right now! For fuck's sake, act like a goddamn professional, you pissant little bastard!"

Two piercing eyes, strong and defiant, bite back at Santa Ana, and they pull at his spine with Death's bony grip. A single thin bead of sweat runs down his brow. He flicks the droplet off before the shadowy figure inside notices his shaken bravado.

"Hurry it up, kid." Santa Ana orders again, in a softer tone. "We've got a job to do."

The young warrior struts out of the cart at a slow pace. Unlike his partners' more dramatic exits, his steps are gentler and patient. He is a solitary young man—a mere boy treading on the bridge of manhood. He appears to be a short decade older than Rubí, yet his body is battle-scarred, signs of a veteran warrior. His most profound scar runs from his upper right brow, down over his cheek like a crack over a diamond.

Rubí notices the young warrior staring at her. She pulls away from her father, and their eyes lock for an infinite second. Both become isolated within a white realm of snow. The stranger's air of trauma mesmerizes her. His eyes sheen with self-hate, but Rubí divines the entombed tortured soul, and she can overhear the silent tragedy that yearns to scream out from its tomb.

She shivers, and she will ponder on this moment for years to come.

Osvaldo pulls Rubí back behind him. His face distorts with palpable revulsion. The bounty killer's green attire, tucked underneath a bomber jacket, reveals his true grain. And the crest above the right chest pocket of the tattered jacket, a skull woven in a pattern of black and white, vindicates Osvaldo's suspicions—this boy is a mutant. But he's no ordinary mutant. He belongs to an untried, but reputable warrior class from Genesis. A warrior class Osvaldo has heard mentioned by a foreboding title—the *Calavera Warriors.*

His name is Xolo. Mutant, warrior, and outcast of Genesis.

••••
——

The bounty killers and their liaisons travel via carriage through the winding frozen dirt road. It is a slow trip. The unnatural climate has claimed all Berumbo's horses in a glacial death and oxen are used in their stead. Their thick hides bear the bitter cold better than horses, but the beasts are bulkier and slower.

"Did you guys get a look at that girl? Oh yes, she's a fine slice of jailbait." Savani said in a hoarse, raspy voice.

"Savani . . . why don't you shut the fuck up?" Santa Ana said with a hard-boiled tone. "Her dad hears any of this filth you're purring and, well, he might just cut our contract. And there goes our bounty. A nice little sum I'll be damned to lose because of that goddamn rabid cock of yours. I'm warning you, perv, any funny business, and I ain't wasting a thought on castrating you."

"Fuck the contract. Fuck the bounty. Girl's a much better prey and her maidenhood a more gratifying bounty." Savani salivates. "I wonder if she's ripe enough already—pissing blood and all. Huh, makes no difference. She'll bleed good once I get working on her."

Santa Ana cocks a pistol and pivots the barrel over Savani's crotch. The lecherous bastard falls silent. "I said shut the fuck up. Go on, spit out another wisecrack. I promise you; you'll bleed like a little girl too."

"Cock blocking queer." Savani snarls.

Santa Ana has made his point and returns the pistol back into its holster. He turns to the watchful and mute mutant. "And what about you, kid? Got anything to say?"

Xolo doesn't answer. He instead turns a heavy gaze to Salvatore and Osvaldo at the driver's box. Rubí is tucked between them. Salvatore commands the lead line, and every few swerves, Xolo snatches Osvaldo shooting him a disagreeable sneer. The mutant knows both men speak about him.

"I'm telling you, *compadre*. He's one of those perversions of the clay from Genesis. The entire town's going to go on a riotous hoot when they see us waltzing in with that stain on our backs." Osvaldo catches Xolo eyeing him with mutual interest. Neither of them blink, nor does Osvaldo care if his cruel remarks are heard. He turns back to Salvatore. "Jesus H. Christ. What are we going to do? His kind aren't welcomed in town. Sight of him makes me want to hurl my guts out."

"Pipe down, Oz." Salvatore hisses. "We've both seen what those mutants are capable of. The last thing we want is to provoke him. What did you expect from the guild anyway? Didn't you say this Neza is an expatriate?"

Salvatore dwells on his initial hesitancy to contract the bounty killers. The guild is renowned for granting amnesty to criminals for the greater good. Salvatore's honorable stance considers such a sanction a contempt-ible compromise in civility. But his hesitancy was fleeting, and he reeked of panicked sweat. Salvatore wipes his brow clean, and rakes a claw over his curly, red beard.

"You've forgotten all too easily, Oz; this was your idea. He's a means to an end, and we've to tolerate his unpleasantness until the dark deed is done. Besides, there are so few of us left to raise grievances about this perversion of the clay."

"I do hate to agree with you on this one, Sal." Osvaldo pouts and slackens his shoulders. "What has this curse driven us to? Consorting with perversions and bastards to evade damnation. I now pray for two things, *compadre*—may the perversion die tomorrow."

After a three-hour trek, the carriage reaches Berumbo's cobblestone roads.

The oxen plow through the snow dunes with great strain, and their burdensome task ends when Salvatore whips the lead line. They arrive at the doorsteps of Osvaldo's business—*El Sapo's Inn*. The group dismounts from the carriage, and slogs toward the inn's doors. A stocky man hops through the snow towards them. He is Osvaldo's manservant, Esteban.

"Welcome home boss." Esteban howls. "Nights sure are getting colder, not sure how much longer the oxen can take it. Two more keeled over stiff cold and dead fifteen minutes before you arrived. We'll be sitting ducks if we stay here any longer. The others had the right idea, boss. Best we desert this accursed wasteland and make ways to the big city before we too freeze to death."

"With a little faith, by day's end tomorrow,

we won't have to." Osvaldo replies. "I can trust you to stay with us until then, right?"

"Sure thing, boss." Esteban catches a quick glance of the bounty killers making their way through the inn's doors. "Is that them over there, Berumbo's would-be heroes?"

"You're on the sauce again, Esteban." Osvaldo yells back while making his way toward the inn. "What have I told you before? There are no more heroes left in this world, just condemned men and their monsters."

Esteban grunts and rushes the oxen back to the stables before the preternatural cold eats them away.

The bounty killers and their liaisons blast through the mahogany doors. The outside squall follows them inside and brushes the frost clear off their shoulders. They stampede to the check-in counter where a petite, stocky woman stands attentive.

"Oh, hello." The plum woman gives the bounty killers a cheeky welcome. "Come in quickly now. Come, come now, don't prance about like little swans on the pond, not when you're built like oxen." She marches past Salvatore and Osvaldo and closes the doors with a loud thud. "Let's keep those garish winds outside where they belong, shall we."—she then wobbles back behind the counter.

The woman fluffs her short-titian curls, dips a quill on the inkpot, and addresses the bounty killers. "Merry salutations and welcome to our humble little town. I am Paciencia Eleadora Barrio, mistress of this here inn. Paciencia means patience, though I reserve very little of it. So, chip-chip, twinkle your toes on over here, one at a time. I'll be jotting down your names here on our guestbook before I issue each of you a room key."

Santa Ana is the first to register his name. He removes his *vaquero* hat and brushes the single ashen feather woven on its rim with playful fingers. He speaks to Paciencia with utmost respect. "Alonso Severino de Santa Ana at your service, ma'am. Killing's the game at the price of a pretty penny, and may I be so bold as to say, you're quite the pretty penny yourself. The Lucky Kid they call me. Why? Because I always get my bounty, whether it be villain or dame. Pleasure to make your acquaintance."

"Keep those trousers of yours strapped

tight, your machismo display is wasted on me," Paciencia snips. She scribbles Santa Ana's name on the guestbook with a forceful dab. "I'm a happily married woman and my Oz is the only man who shall ever butter up my voluptuous curves on the nightly."

Paciencia hands him the key to Room 16.

Santa Ana walks away, the plumpish woman's scorn leaving him aroused.

Osvaldo bites down his lip. The Lucky Kid passes around him without worry and is ignorant of the wrath he has just baited. Paciencia is a military brat, a warrior who's been toughened in the throes of war. The scents of boiling mud, blood and shrapnel embattled her body, but never wilted her blunt wit or sympathy for strangers. Osvaldo knows better than to have tried to step in and uphold his wife's honor—Paciencia would've been quite miffed and insulted.

Salvatore pats Osvaldo on the shoulder, always impressed by the woman he was wise in making his wife. "I think she'll be okay by herself, Oz. We best go forward with the other arrangements in the meantime."

"Aye, I know she will." Osvaldo said. He hesitates until Paciencia cocks him a brow. "If that woman doesn't kill me in the sack, that mouth of hers surely will."

Salvatore and Osvaldo march to the inn's conference room. Savani's eyes remain glued to a lagging Rubí. Xolo nudges him and Savani hears Paciencia calling him to the counter.

"I hear you, woman!" Savani drools.

"Oh my, aren't you a darling little terror. Must've been quite a feat for your mother to love you so." Paciencia taunts. "Now, come along, no time for pleasantries. Spit out your name."

"Savani. Vicenzo Francesco Savani." Savani growls. "Remember it bitch. Mine is the face death will be wearing when it comes calling for you."

"Is that so? Hm, well, I'll be sure to recite my rosary every night henceforth." Paciencia said unamused. "Savani? You wouldn't happen to be related to an Alphonse Favier Savani?"

"Huh? Yeah, I know him. You know my big brother too?" Savani snorts. "Goes by El Chupacabra these days. Last thing I heard; he's raising some hell down south. I'd join him in the orgy of blood if I didn't love hating the fucker so much."

"That monster killed a good friend of mine

nigh two months ago." Paciencia said. Her grip on the quill buckles tighter and her knuckles turn ivory white. "Her name was Phoebe, and she was a sweet darling. She went to the big city to tend to her ailing mother. One week, the doctors told her, before she'd go in peace. Chupacabra, or whatever that bastard calls himself now, didn't give poor Phoebe the grace of two days with her mother. He followed her home one late afternoon and forced his way into the apartment. That beast raped her till she bled dry, all while her bedridden mother watched helpless in horror. Phoebe was defiled like a dog, gutted like a fish, and her mother died soon after of a broken heart."

"Poor lassie. I suppose you half expect me to sniff a tear or two for your dead little friend. But fibbing's never been my vice—I make no lies. Murdering, raping, that's my kind of fun. So, here's the raw truth." Savani leans down towards Paciencia. His lolling tongue caresses the tips of his buffed fangs. "Little whore got off easy. My brother usually milks the fear out of his bitches for weeks on end, 'til they're nothing but limp dolls. He enjoys watching the joy escape from their eyes. Shite gets him off every time."

Paciencia slams the guestbook shut. She never blinks. Her body never quakes. And her eyes remain tearless. "You're too late. I've laid to rest the memory of my dearest Phoebe. But at least I now know who and what you are—*Mosca*, the Fly. That's what they call you back in the big city, isn't it? You slimy, shit-eating little maggot. I warn you, touch or ogle my little goddaughter again and I'll personally divorce your head from the rest of your body."

Savani laughs off Paciencia's threat and takes the key to Room 14.

"You know, I'm feeling a bit dog-tired. The trip to this piss stain was long and boring. I'm going to head to my room now and get some much-needed rest." He turns to Xolo. "Tell Santa Ana I'm out for the night, will you, kid?"

Xolo says nothing. He retains his silent and stolid composure.

"Well? Don't just stand there." Paciencia calls out to Xolo. "Step up to the counter so I can jot down your name and hand you a room key." She reopens the guestbook and dips the quill in the inkpot like a peeved woodpecker. Her eyes flinch when she notices Xolo's youthful face. "Dearie me, you're nothing but a wee babe. Heavens and hells, I can't even begin to imagine what's your story and I don't think I care to know. Your friend back there got my panties all twisted in a knot. Alright, hon, let us have your name now."

"Xolo." He whispers under his breath. His voice is soft and timid.

"Xolo? What a peculiar name and quite fitting if I say so. We do live in peculiar times, after all." Paciencia starts penning his name on the page. "You got a last name to go with that lonesome one, hon?"

"Guevara, and, um, he's not my friend," Xolo adds. "Neither of them is. And the name's spelled X-o-l-o, like the naked dog. The, um, Xolo—itz—uh—itz . . ."—he stutters.

"The Xoloitzcuintle." Paciencia interjects. "Yes, I'm quite familiar with the not-so-bashful breed. Odd name for one so shy, I might add."

"My mother, um . . . she, um . . ." Xolo mumbles, "she named me so to honor them— the naked dogs. It's the only thing I've ever learned about her."

"Orphans can rarely be so fortunate." Paciencia deduces Xolo's rootlessness with ease. She slams the guestbook shut and darts him a sleuthing glance. "Don't mind me saying so, hon, but I'm having a hard time reading you.

The other two sons of whores I get. You, on the other hand, strike me differently. You've partaken of what people like us call *la danza de los diablos*. The garish scar scratched down your face reveals that much. I ask now from one warrior to another, but you're a mutant from Genesis, aren't you?"

Xolo nods. His hardened glower loosens, and he exposes an inner, maimed vulnerability. Paciencia's scrutiny differs from Osvaldo's bigotry—she offers Xolo the mutual respect shared among honorable warriors.

"Oh my, my Oz must've shit himself mad when he discovered this," Paciencia chortles. "Pay him and Salvatore no mind, hon. But I must demand that you understand us. We're not like the rest in this backwater town. We three have a mutual history with your peoples' Great Schism, and we've borne witness, firsthand, to your renowned predisposition for apocalyptic warfare. Though we survived, we've not forgotten."

"We were bred for war," Xolo retorts calmly. "We were shaped from man's clay to war with his eldest progeny, man's hubris and avarice upraised from the earth's ore. Our martyrdom was unwavering and, nevertheless, our honor went unrewarded. Now we claim our sovereignty, and man grows fearful and envious, as do all gods stripped of godhood."

"How poetic, if somewhat insulting." Paciencia twirls the key to Room 9 between her stubby fingers. "I admit, we've made many grave mistakes raising you, kids. Then again, parenthood is a series of fuck ups. Did you come up with that little piece yourself?"

"No." Xolo replies with a heavy breath. "My queen, she, she would often recite it to me during history lessons."

"Ah, Genesis' *Infanta Reina*." Paciencia giggles. "I'm impressed. She certainly exceeds her infant years. Quite the little prickly pear, too, so I've heard."

"She's not my queen." Xolo growls. He snatches the room key off Paciencia's dancing fingers. "I—I'm sorry. I meant the former queen, her sister."—he pleads, ashamed.

"Isabella." Paciencia mouths and takes two steps back. She gropes her chest with a single hand. "You knew Queen Isabella, *la Victoriosa*? I met her once, long ago, when I was a much riper, smaller cantaloupe. Isabella, huh. A proud one she was, a fierce warrior too, and stubborn as a mule when it came to her people.

I, um, I heard about the regicide, two years back, I believe. I—I'm sorry for your peoples' loss, hon. They ever find her assassin?"

"I–I wouldn't know." Xolo stutters. The question unsettles him. "I've been away from home for a long time now."

"I see." Paciencia sighs. She gives him a stern, suspicious look. "Down the hall to the right, second door to your left, you'll find our conference room. Now, chip-chip, off with you, hon. We got a banquet waiting for you, as is custom with these morbid affairs."

Xolo walks away but stops mid-step down the hallway. He pauses and turns around to face Paciencia. "Ma'am, thank you for your kindness."—he says to her.

"Consider it a warrior's courtesy, hon," Paciencia said with a small smile, and bowed his way. "And what does it matter what we are, when in the end we all bleed alike."

"We don't know what the creature is exactly. A demon, a monster . . . such primitive super-stitions are crazy to perceive and much more difficult to accept as true." Salvatore explains to

Santa Ana with a rasp in his voice. "But that's really not important—"

The room falls silent as Xolo walks through the doors. He ignores both Salvatore and Osvaldo's scowls and saunters across the room. He sits beside Santa Ana, and watches the Lucky Kid take a big bite from a turkey leg and wash it down with a large chalice of red wine. Xolo scans the banquet; it is an adequate, contingent, last meal for the bounty killers—men condemned to a random fate. He poaches a single biscuit and nibbles on finger portions.

"Where's Savani?" Santa Ana burps.

"He ran off to bed to lick his wounds." Xolo replies under his breath. "The inn's mistress handed him his nuts good."

Santa Ana scoffs and then laughs.

"Gentlemen, if you're finished, I'd like to continue with the formalities?" Salvatore interjects with a stern voice. Santa Ana nods with a cocky smirk. "What the creature is, is an inconsequential detail, but there are a few certainties we do know about it. Firstly, it is an effective killer. The creature swam through the shadows like a shark and slaughtered sixteen of our strongest men within minutes. The last thing you've witnessed for yourselves. Its mere existence has cursed our home and the surrounding mountains with an undying winter. Many have fled south to the city already. We few who've stayed behind are unwilling to let our town rot away to nothing."

"If this food's the best your town has got to offer," Santa Ana sucks his teeth, "then, in my opinion, this hunk of shit ain't worth saving. Why trouble yourselves hiring degenerates like us, then? Your town's unexceptional, just another worthless fucking wart lost far up civilization's asshole. No one will even notice when it's gone or miss it."

"Hey, you can't talk to us like that. You're under contract." Osvaldo barks in protest.

"There's where you're wrong, *compadre*. Our contract prohibits me and these two other eunuchs from harming you and yours. I am free to speak whatever the fuck I please." Santa Ana lets off a wry laugh. He then pierces a mocking glare on Osvaldo. "And if we're being frank, gents, I'd rather be plowing my cock so far up your wife's asshole that the bitch's mouth will be foaming out cum like a rabid dog. It's more emasculating than insulting when you think about it—you two fucks are paying me for this."

"You son of a bitch! How dare you speak of her in such a vulgar matter!" Osvaldo jumps up and charges straight toward Santa Ana but stops short. Xolo gets between him and Santa Ana, and he holds a narrow, oblong sliver of obsidian in his right hand. Osvaldo eyes the sliver of obsidian with caution. He scowls at Xolo and sits back down without uttering another word.

"That's quite enough Santa Ana." Salvatore commands. "Disrespect Oz's wife again, and I'll terminate our contract with you."

Santa Ana laughs and motions Xolo to sit back down.

"I'm sorry. I joked, honest to God." Santa Ana said in a feigned tone. "No more games then. Let's discuss our fee now. Salvation's going to cost you a cornucopia of riches. You got all that ready for us?"

Salvatore shares a sidelong look with Osvaldo. They nod in agreement.

"Good." Santa Ana's face creases with a sinister smile. "I'd like my eyes to touch the promised fortunes before the kill."

Salvatore walks toward a wooden armoire. He pulls out the key from his pockets and unbuckles the lock to swing open its copper doors. Two separate leather sacks are fat to the seam with gold and silver coins, and thirty twenty-ounce jars of honey are stacked in neat order on the bottom shelves. Santa Ana dismisses the fatty sacks and reaches out to one of the honey jars instead. Honeybee populations are luxuries, a nigh mythological species.

Santa Ana opens the jar. He dips a finger and takes a taste of the honey with a broad smile. He then seals the jar, sits it back on the shelf, and returns to his seat and meal. "The honey alone is worth half a mil gold coin. You're fools to give away such wealth."

"Fools? You think us fools?" Salvatore asks, peeved. "Tell me something, Santa Ana, how far out from the waystation were you before you penetrated the snow?"

Santa Ana cocks a quizzical look. "I'm not too sure—eight, ten miles."

"Last week it was nowhere near the waystation or nearby roads." Salvatore adds with a trembling voice. His eyes quiver, too. "And two months before, that impure whiteout moved past the ridgeline and devoured all Berumbo. Seven months further back, the tower that birthed this Shark Monster never existed—this accursed thing is not of our world, and it won't be long before everyone from everywhere can feel the frigid curse claw all around their faces."

Salvatore locks the armoire. "And who better to alleviate our sins than men who tread on the road to perdition?" He nods to Osvaldo and both men walk out the doors. "Enjoy your meal gentlemen, it may be your last. Tomorrow be wary of the shadows—you won't see Death's eyes until it comes calling."

Santa Ana scoffs at the shutting doors. The Lucky Kid is left wordless and continues to gorge himself with turkey and wine.

Xolo kept to himself throughout the entire exchange. He prefers a duel of blades over one of words. The mutant's eyes swept across every corner of the conference room, and he noticed that Salvatore's daughter was absent from the room.

"Where was the girl?" Xolo asks Santa Ana.

"Hm?" Santa Ana lifts a surprised brow at Xolo. "What girl?" He chugs some more wine. "Oh, the one Savani was eyeing like a chew toy. The girl turns out to be good with her hands. Old man Sal sent her out to the barn to milk the cows before bed. She's not my type, far too young, but I won't lie. Savani's got good taste.

She'll ripen to a fox. Why do you ask? Fancy her, do you?"

A dark thought crosses Xolo's mind. The girl is alone, and Savani is out there without a leash. He gets up and moves towards the doors with great haste.

"Where you off to, kid?" Santa Ana yells, spitting out chunks of turkey.

"To take a piss." Xolo answers back and storms off into the halls.

Rubí enjoys milking the cows very little. She can never get used to the smell of manure and cow hide. But, helping hands are scarce as of late at Berumbo and everyone, from the young and old, must pull their weight.

The milk cylinder holds up to ten buckets of milk. Rubí is unsure of how many gallons that is, but she pumps ten buckets from the cow, Attila, and ten buckets she dumps into the milk cylinder. If the accursed weather offers any blessings, it saves her the need to drag the milk cylinder indoors to the kitchen freezer. The outdoors is a better freezer either way.

Rubí finishes her chore and takes in some

light reading. She keeps her bum on the stool and face glued to the book—a historical account of the bohemian Cuckoo Meadows. Yet, her still eyes do not absorb the words on the pages because her thoughts are elsewhere—on Berumbo's future, her guilt for having survived the massacre over Santiago, and on the mutant, Xolo.

Rubí has never met a mutant before. Her knowledge of Genesis and its mutant populace is limited to the town library's sparse books on its century and half history. Her father and godparents have histories with Genesis, but rarely do they discuss anything about mutants and their involvement during the waning years of Genesis' civil war—the Great Schism. Their views on Genesis and its mutants are suspicious and bitter, compounded by their fears over their preternatural abilities.

They are perversions of the clay, the proverbial darkness that dwells in our souls. Grown from our hubris, we've engineered the perfect vessel for Death to inhabit. —Osvaldo would often tell her.

But from the moment Rubí locked eyes with Xolo back at the waystation, she understood the shortsightedness of her uncle's biased judgment. Xolo was unlike the other two. A noble spirit gleamed off those tortured eyes, and a heroic fury roiled behind them. Rubí wonders if Xolo sensed it too—their mutual aloneness.

Rubí becomes isolated in her thoughts, numb to her surroundings. She is blind and deaf to the predator who lurks in the chilled shadows and who undresses her with titillating hunger.

"Hiya there, little bug." Savani hisses and emerges out of the shadows.

Rubí jolts up but doesn't run away. Although Savani disgusts her to the gut, she is not afraid of him. She won't give him that satisfaction.

"My, oh my. What's a pretty bug such as yourself doing out here all alone in the cold? I bet you're very cold, little bug. Shivering under that coat and fur, I wager." Savani struts towards her, fingers dancing in the empty air. He is eager to touch her, eager to nibble her neck. "Come here, little bug. I'll keep you warm. Oh yes, I will."

She's too afraid, but not for herself. Rubí knows her father will hear her cries, and he would do the predictable thing—come to her aid. Salvatore is neither a warrior nor a fighter.

He is a scholar and intellectual. Savani will bludgeon him to death, Rubí is certain of this. She will not scream and keep her father away and safe.

"Come now, little bug, no need to be shy with me. It's no fun if you don't scream." Savani drools. "You smell good, like a new spring morning. You're ripe, girl, just the way I like 'em. I wonder . . . how sweet the nectar, down there, tastes like."

Savani attempts to claw Rubí but snatches a fistful of her long, black hair instead. He misses her by a few inches, and she falls back, right next to the stool. Savani lunges at her, but Rubí grabs the stool and smashes it up against his crotch. Savani slumps backward with a high-pitched whine. The jingling chains and Attila's terrified mooing are snuffed by the howling winds.

No one hears them. Rubí is on her own.

"You, fucking little bitch!" Savani wheezes. "I'm going to shaft you 'til every fucking hole in your body bleeds. Fucking little cunt!"

Rubí jumps to her feet, hops around Savani, and attempts to run away. But Savani grabs her right foot, and he flings her to the floor. Savani growls and rises to his feet, hungry to satiate his anger and lust for blood—he will mend this humiliation.

"I'm going to beat female pains down on you, girl!" Savani growls with drool seeping between his fangs. He swings a clenched fist, but . . . Savani's fist never hammers Rubí's face.

A firm grip interrupts their scuffle—Xolo has arrived, and he holds on to Savani's fisted wrist!

"Lay off, freak, unless you want my cock up your asshole instead!" Savani barks.

Xolo says nothing and tightens his grip on Savani's wrist. The raving Savani falls to his knees, agony rains down his eyes as tears form. Xolo never strays his eyes off the whimpering Savani.

He addresses Rubí with a calm voice. "What are you waiting for, girl? Go on, get back to your father—now."

The soft click of a pistol halts Rubí mid-toe. Santa Ana hovers the barrel over her chest. "Not so fast, little bug." He pulls out his second pistol and aims it straight at Savani's skull. "I warned you Savani. No funny business or I ain't wasting a thought on castrating you."

BOOM! —The bullet whizzes past Savani's

right ear. The blast pollutes his ears with a piercing ring.

"Lucky for you, job's loot is too good to pass by. I'm going to need all of you tomorrow, testicles and cock." Santa Ana turns to Xolo. "Alright, let him go, kid. Next time, tell me what the fuck's going on instead of going lone wolf on the situation. Do you understand? Quit trying to play hero, kid. Role doesn't suit you, not when we both know what you really are."

Xolo scowls at Santa Ana. He tightens his grip on Savani until a soft crunch goes off. Savani whimpers like a pathetic child. After a brief standoff with the Lucky Kid, the mutant loosens his grip.

Savani collapses to his knees. He rubs his aching wrist and ringing ear. "I'll kill you for this freak. Guild Master Neza ain't here to protect you this time around."

"Savani, shut the fuck up." Santa Ana orders without pity. He turns to Rubí, pistol still hovering over her chest. "Not a word about this to your pops. Whisper a peep and I promise you, we'll be gone by morning. Don't worry, we won't kill you or whoever else is left in this piss stain of a town. But whatever is out there, in that cave or whatever, will. You don't want to be responsible for dooming your entire town, do you girl?"

Rubí shakes her head.

"Good girl. Now get on out here." Santa Ana waves her away with the pistol.

Rubí scurries away. She reaches the barn's back door and turns around. Xolo watches her, and once again, their eyes embrace from a distance.

"Thank you." She tells him, then disappears behind the door.

Xolo is stunned. His stern gaze broadens to surprise. She is the first person to have ever thanked him.

CHAPTER 3
ORPHANS UNDER THE NIGHT SUN

April 13, 2222, roughly 3:00 a.m.

Rubí always waits three hours after the last light clicks off before sneaking out of her bedroom window, but tonight takes a bit longer. The last light clicks off at around 3:00 a.m.—four hours later than usual. Her lateness is a minor hiccup. She has indulged this late-night getaway for three months now and has mastered the routine down to a ritual. Either way, she was already swaddled in her winter clothes hours ahead of the last light turning off. Rubí sneaks toward the window but halts mid-step and swirls back into her room. She rummages through the dresser for the one sacred item— her favorite pink scarf. She almost forgot all about it. The cold air's gust runs tepid across her face and melts upon her touch, and the scarf offers her a different sort of comfort.

The scarf is a bandage. It cloaks the grotesqueness branded right below the right side of her neck. The mark of melted flesh is of her doing, a naïve act of penance spurred by Salvatore's sin, and her desperate yearning for a mother's love. A foolish plead from a foolish girl made to an unforgiving, proud woman; the scar never did cure Rubí's heartbreak at learning she is an orphan, an unknowing usurper to Charlotte's love. To her immediate regret, the scar transcribed Salvatore's betrayal and Charlotte's abandonment over her flesh—an unforgettable memory that will haunt and shame her until death claims her.

Rubí slides the bedroom window open, and the frost snickers with every rising inch. She crawls out, careful not to slip on the verglas that lays invisible over the roof of their two-story home. Should Salvatore ever learn about her moonlit activities, he would never understand and lock her away down in the basement. *"It is for your own good"*—he would say to her. He is a loving father who means well, but Rubí has grown restless underneath Salvatore's protective eye, his gaze becoming more unbearable and suffocating after Santiago's death.

But her restlessness is inborn, probably from her unknown, true heritage. Berumbo's banality and conformity to halcyon days does not suit her rebellious spirit. Many spring nights, Rubí would stare out to the stars from her bedroom window, and dream about undertaking a great adventure. But at times, even dreaming becomes tiresome. Berumbo is her prison, her inescapable island, and she is alone and often misunderstood. She looks to the stars yearning to reach a world she cannot touch.

This night is different though. There will be no stargazing for her. Not that there are any stars to admire. The curse has all but robbed Berumbo of its fertility, and now it too has robbed it of the stars.

Rubí tiptoes around her parent's bedroom window. Long ago, even after dark, their angry voices would roar like thunder from behind, drowning out Rubí's gentle sobs. Times are darker, and they've long exhausted themselves to silence. She climbs down the balcony's vine lattice, shattering the frozen vines into icicles. She reaches the ground and scampers down the empty cobblestone road.

The howling winds accompany her throughout the solitary trek onto the town square. Rubí struggles to kick up a good pace with the sack she carries flung over her shoulders. The sack is stuffed with scraps from the bounty killers' banquet, and she hid it in her mother's crystalized rose garden after returning from the inn with her father. The scraps are for the only friend she has in Berumbo. She stops for a minute at the town square fountain and scouts the barren town. This white wasteland is Berumbo, and she cannot believe it.

She shivers with worry.

Rubí cradles herself and she ponders what this mysterious chill down the nape of her neck could possibly be. The horrified, frozen faces of the fountain koi do not terrify her a bit, and the fountain's stone statue of Berumbo's mythical nagual guardian, the eaglelike Tizoc, does little to offer her comfort. Fear creeps into her heart as it did the night her brother, Santiago, died. Berumbo suffers a slow death, and they've placed its salvation on the hands of damnable men.

A mile out of Berumbo's main gates, along

the eastern main road, a frail, spindly tree sits atop a cliff. The preternatural winds flay its bark without remorse and have stripped every leaf off its boughs, down to its dancing twigs. The tree's tomorrows are no more certain than Berumbo's. Nevertheless, the tree's vigilance is unyielding. Even when the baleful air threatens to smite it down, the tree remains unbowed and contorted sideways with its roots clinging to the cliff's soil by the tip. Rubí finds such stubbornness honorable and brave, much like the jaguar cub that waits for her underneath the hollow, hidden behind the curtain of unearthed roots.

Before the snow began its slow crawl across the ridgeline the jaguars were the first creatures the curse chased away in fear. Without the jaguars, Berumbo's townspeople fell prey to superstition, and the Shark Monster's fathomless hunger for carnage. Then, naturally, when Rubí and her uncle Osvaldo discovered a female jaguar raiding *El Sapo's Inn's* barn for food on a Sunday morning, three months ago, they became stiff with bewilderment. The jaguar was the largest Rubí had ever seen roam the mountains. Her fur was white and shimmered like moonlight, and a calf laid slack, pinched at the neck between its fangs. The frightened animal leapt over them and beetled off from the barn onto the eastern road with its kill. Osvaldo yelled to Salvatore, and both men gave chase to it, armed with rifles. A strange worry for the jaguar's wellbeing bewitched Rubí, and she ran behind them, out of sheer instinct and much to her father's later scorn.

The jaguar was cornered, shot, and killed by Salvatore on this very cliff where the tree sits. Rubí mourned for the jaguar from that day to this.

Later that night, three hours after the last light clicked off, Rubí revisited the cliff. She took a stone about the size of a melon and inscribed the words "Moon Goddess" on it with chalk. Rubí thought it the moral thing to do, to leave a gravestone to honor the innocent slain by the Shark Monster's curse.

"Whatever were you doing out here all alone?" —the question just touched her thoughts when a gentle mewling called out to her from underneath the tree's slant. She dug and clawed her way through the roots until she reached the hidden hollow where the black jaguar cub cried for his slain mother.

"If the cold doesn't kill him, then he will grow strong and feed on our livestock. Small or not, he's

a threat to our own survival"—Salvatore's voice echoed.

Rubí knew her father would've had the poor cub slain after dismissing her pleas for mercy as childish naivety.

The cub was made an orphan much like she was when Salvatore rescued her from a similar snowy cradle, and what could she do if not offer the cub the same mercy Salvatore demonstrated to her thirteen years ago.

Rubí squeezes through the furrow while tugging the sack behind her. She enters the warm hollow beneath the tree.

"Little one, little one, you can come out now. I'm here." Rubí calls to the jaguar cub. "You're going to love tonight's scraps—turkey and ham."—she adds while laying out the small feast.

Two little blue eyes, cold like ice, dance behind the shadows. The jaguar cub leaps out with a wagging tail and springs towards the grub. Rubí scratches his soft head and looks to the purring cub with a smile. She reaches a hand inside the sack again and pulls out the wooden jaguar Salvatore gave her the night of Santiago's death. And the second she lays it on the ground, the cub pounces on it with gnawing fangs.

"Hey, don't do that, you little troublemaker. I brought it here to liven up your loneliness—it's not food." Rubí chides with a giggle. She pries the cub off the wooden figure, turns him on his back, and rubs his ashen tummy. "Three months. That's how long I've played mother to you. But I've not named you yet. Why is that do you suppose?" she asks the purring cub. "The easy thing to say is that I'm not very good at picking names . . . I remember wanting to name my little brother Arnulfo—what a terrible name. I was so jealous of him, and now all I can do is . . . miss him."

Rubí trembles. She hugs herself and lets off a low laugh that fades into a sad sigh. She continues. "The other thing isn't so easy to admit or say, really. One day, probably as soon as tomorrow, you'll grow big and strong, strong enough to care for and protect these mountains from curses and monsters . . . even from me. Your coat will grow dark like the night and your eyes will shine like the moon, like the night sun." Rubí pouts on the last thought. "Balam," she utters, "that shall be your name, little one . . . Balam. I wonder . . . if when we meet again in the years after you've grown and left this hollow, will your heart conquer your instincts? And will you remember me then, Balam?" she asks in a doleful tone and with watery eyes.

The cub suddenly rolls over on his paws, and his tiny ears and tail perk up, alert. Someone or something treads outside in the snow. Rubí keeps the cub calm with the wooden jaguar figure, and she peeps through the small clearing between the roots. Her heart races. She half-expects to see her father outside waiting for her, with a stern lecture prepped and recited. To Rubí's surprise and relief, it isn't Salvatore, but the mutant, Xolo.

Xolo stands silent with a hard glare piercing the impenetrable darkness before him. He remains oblivious to Rubí's phantom presence under the tree and in the company of an orphan jaguar cub. Twin thunderclouds churn behind his unblinking glare, testament to the nightmares that haunt him with no end. He reaches for the narrow, oblong sliver of obsidian he had threatened Osvaldo with earlier. Xolo is a mutant, a warrior of Genesis, gifted with preternatural abilities bestowed upon his race by mankind's vanity and resolve. The sliver of obsidian is a conduit—a weapon—through which he exploits these hibernating gifts.

Xolo concentrates on the totality of his preternatural gifts and a small green burst of energies rivulet down his right arm to the hand that clutches the sliver of obsidian. The obsidian's solidity collapses and transmutes into a long, broad ebony *macuahuitl* studded with green prismatic blades around the edges. The elaborate skull design stenciled at the hilt's center vibrates with rings of the same energies that summoned it.

The *macuahuitl* is a perfect weapon for Xolo—good for shredding, piercing, and clubbing. Xolo tips the *macuahuitl's* stone flake point on the ground and twirls in a spin, issuing a streak of dust and snow. He stiffens his clutch round the hilt tighter and pulls back the club-like sword. Snowflakes pelt the smooth, black mirror surface, melting down to crystal beads that thin into smoking steam. Xolo shuts his eyes and takes a deep breath. His heart beats to the *macuahuitl's* volcanic thrum.

He reawakens and pierces the air, only to pull back the *macuahuitl* in a defensive stance.

Xolo then cuts through the air again and again. The mutant engages in *la danza de los diablos*—the dance of warfare. Xolo pulls the weapon in close, twirls it, and cements the tip, six o'clock, onto the frozen earth.

He kneels on one knee to meditate, but the pelting snow bogs his calmness down into a brood. Old wounds bleed with a deluge of undying memories. The hilt's skull stares back at him, and he looks back into a shattered mosaic that gleams with blinding light. He drowns in grief and madness.

Xolo closes his eyes and gives in to the mosaic's pull. The deluge of memories pulls him back to Genesis' islands. Then, after nigh two years in exile . . . he is home again.

Genesis . . . several years in the past.

The solecism of an incessant civil war, the Great Schism, has forever deformed Genesis' once perfect gene pool. Mestizos, a new mutant breed, is born from *la cruce de razas*—the crossbreed of mutant and human bloodlines.

For Genesis' mutant populace, genetics is everything, and this newborn mutant breed defiles their culture and dilutes their genetic pedigree. But Queen Isabella is of a different opinion. These mutts, these ill-made orphans, who killed their mothers to come into this cruel existence are meant to teach them humility and curb their suicidal prides. Then there is the reality of their depleted warrior caste. Queen Isabella, in her desperation, then decreed that these mestizos should be denied the courtesy of innocence, and their genotypes gauged and categorized into Genesis' resurrected Eagle and Jaguar Knighthoods.

Xolo, age five, is among these mestizo orphans.

He stands under a pillar of light, afraid and ignorant of the events occurring around him. A prideful man—the old adversary—apprises him with a contemptible sneer. They branded Xolo an undesirable.

"Weak. So very weak." The bloodless man whispers. Xolo's gentle sobs inspire no sympathy from the man. It only further strengthens his revulsion for this mestizo, this impure mutt. *"Weak and pathetic, it would appear. He is perhaps the worst of these strays and mutts. These perversions serve no purpose within our noble ranks, except, perhaps, as slaves."*

The man's cruel taunts continue, fading into distant echoes.

Two broadswords clash, grass blades dance with the wind and Xolo snatches the ever-observant emerald eyes. They gleam with compassion.

Everything then fades, drowned in the shrills of pandemonium and death.

Genesis' cradling oceans swirl onto whirlpools and the trinity of islands quake beneath the preternatural pull of a resolved man—the *Howler Monkey Warrior*—who'd become corrupt under a moon that sheened red like blood. His golden, mad eyes burn with a fateful fire, and the islands fall toward the skies. Genesis' people devour one another in a stampede of fear and confusion. Throngs of bodies hurdle themselves off the edges of the rising islands, falling weightless onto a watery death. The screams continue and Xolo bears witness to a person's sins encumber a kingdom with the threat of extinction. Such sins will corrupt him, too, with anger and hate.

Xolo takes up the role of fool and challenges the *Howler Monkey Warrior* blessed with the Terrestrial Fire. His nemesis smiles, delighted to engage the boy in *la danza de los diablos*. He outstretches his right arm, and the sliver of alabaster stone clutched to his hand is consumed by crimson energies, transmuted into a crystal, icebound *macuahuitl.*

Both warriors engage. Their feral screams and clashing *macuahuitls* are then washed away in a white flare.

"We were bred for war," Isabella's voice echoes. *"We were shaped from man's clay to war with his eldest progeny, man's hubris and avarice upraised from the earth's ore. Our martyrdom was unwavering and, nevertheless, our honor went unrewarded. Now we claim our sovereignty, and man grows fearful and envious as do all gods stripped of godhood . . ."*

Two broadswords shriek against one another and sparks drizzle over the grassland.

The years have passed, and Xolo is now age ten. He duels with a beautiful, svelte woman. The long, flowing cream dress wrapped around her lithe body complements her cascading, braided, black hair. "She is an angel"—so Xolo thinks. He snatches her emerald eyes again, and shuns away, bashfully.

Queen Isabella, *la Victoriosa,* sovereign ruler of Genesis, has taken Xolo under her personal tutelage. Xolo is honored that out of Genesis' hundreds of mestizo orphans, she chose him above all others. He never considers the crucial question—the why.

Their broadswords clash, and sparks burst like droplets of rain. Isabella swings the broadsword with the precision and agile speed of a hummingbird. Xolo does his best to fight back but struggles to parry her strikes. He thinks it is easier to fight off lightning than Isabella's unpredictable swings. A misstep or careless distraction will prove the end for him, a lesson learned in blood and even death. For months on end, early at dawn, Xolo has endured Isabella's brutal lessons of combat and warfare by the sword. In a short time, she has shaped this undesirable mutant, this mestizo mutt, into quite an adept swordsman with great promise. But Isabella is the superior warrior, and she is a merciless teacher.

Isabella's moves are weightless and fluid, much like an angel on flight. She dances around Xolo, swinging and jabbing him with the broadsword. Her swings careen through the brushing winds, and her blows are powerful on contact. Xolo continues to parry until the vibration over his broadsword stings his palms. His guard drops, and Isabella grabs him by the hair and flings him to the floor. Xolo drops the broadsword and falls on his back. He is left breathless and groaning in pain. But the lesson isn't over, and Isabella flips the broadsword back near his knees with the tip of her own broadsword.

"Again." Isabella commands, swinging her broadsword in a defensive stance.

Xolo succumbs to the rage he has long subdued. He has become frustrated with his weakness, and rushes her with the broadsword, screaming like a mad beast. His strikes are less disciplined and focused. Isabella parries each blow with ease. She finds an opening between the maddened strike and twirls up in the air to deliver a spearing, downward jab. Xolo blocks it, but the force of the blow sends him flying across the grassland. Isabella's strike is stronger than what he expected, and it would have been a fatal strike had he not blocked it. For a second time, Xolo drops his broadsword and, again, Isabella flips it back near his knees.

"Again." Isabella commands.

The wind howls, and the grass needles whisper. Xolo lifts the broadsword and meditates this time around. He silences the wrath which commands him with ease, and he exhales. He finds peace and resumes his attack. Isabella is pleased. Xolo's attacks are more precise and calculated. The underdog, the same frightened whelp Vargas dismissed with revulsion a few years prior, has evolved into a prodigy through sheer, unyielding will. Now it is she who finds herself parrying.

She smiles.

Isabella attempts another twirling spear attack, but this time, Xolo does not parry it. Instead, he rolls right under her before the attack pierces the earth. Shocked, Isabella gasps. She did not anticipate Xolo's bold move. She is left vulnerable to an attack from behind. Xolo kicks her down. For the first time since their training sessions began, Xolo has the upper hand on Isabella. He moves in for the deathblow. He holds the broadsword toward the clouds. The blade gleams with bubbles of light, and Isabella's emerald eyes petrify the would-be prodigy.

Xolo hesitates and drops the broadsword to his toes. His queen is not pleased.

Isabella scoffs at his show of mercy and, with a soft telekinetic push, sends Xolo flying backwards into the air. He lands face down on the grass and drops the broadsword for a third time. Dazed, Xolo looks up to meet Isabella's downcast, stern eyes with shame. The broadsword's tip pricks his neck.

"Ping. You're dead." Isabella proclaims, disappointed. She throws the broadsword to the side, frustrated. "Is that what you want? To die so easily, to be killed by your own stupidity on the battlefield. You had won. You'd bested me, yet you surrendered that victory for the sake of mercy. Why did you hesitate?"

"I—I couldn't do it." Xolo stutters.

"And why is that? Is it because I'm a woman?" Isabella asks with a wry tone. She waits for an answer. Nothing. She scoffs. "I appreciate your honorable conduct, but on the battlefield, that sort of asinine mentality will earn you a swift death."

"That's not why I hesitated." Xolo blurts. His eyes shy away from her.

"Then why?" Isabella demands.

Xolo hesitates. His voice trembles. "You—You're my friend. When I realized what I've done, I–I couldn't do it. I just couldn't. Milady, forgive me. It's just that I–I . . . you're my Queen."

"That may change one day. Loved ones and even friends can often prove to be your deadliest adversaries." Isabella sighs, reminding herself that Xolo is still a mere boy, an orphan no less. "You're young, Xolo, and you'll do well to mind your history lessons. This will be harder for you to understand than it is for me to explain. My brother, Félix . . . when the war broke out, he sided with our enemies and aided in overthrowing our father, King Ferdinand. My brother committed many atrocities throughout the war. Against his own people, his own family and blood. But our father's love for him never waned.

When the war began to turn in our favor, Félix ordered an armistice by the mysterious tower that sprung from the earth. Father was overjoyed—he'd finally won his son back. We met him by the tower, where he asked—pleaded—for forgiveness. He and father embraced, and . . . and that's when Félix dug his dagger through our father's throat. I watched him die frozen at my heels, not in fear, but disbelief. Father's love for his lone son got him killed, made him forget that Félix was the enemy. Félix, none the wiser, thought that our father's unwilling sacrifice would end the war, sparing hundreds more from the slaughter. He was wrong, and the war raged on. To this day, I still hate myself for ever loving my brother so. You see, Xolo, love can often birth the greatest, most merciless of monsters. Monsters who all too often lure us into death's cold embrace with rueful faces and shameful smiles."

Xolo nods. He picks up the broadsword and gets in a battle stance.

Isabella does the same. "Again."—she commands, and the broadswords resume their clash.

Xolo never managed to best Isabella thereafter.

Noon fell, signaling the end of Isabella's stern lessons, and they now canoe down a canal. Xolo works the paddles while Isabella lays under an umbrella. Xolo remembers. This is his queen's favorite pastime, a leisure canoe ride down Genesis' interconnected canals all to admire the arching tress and blossoming flowers on their way to the marketplace.

His arms are heavy with strain, yet Xolo continues to paddle.

"I spoke with your instructors at the academy earlier this week." Isabella said, rippling the calm waters with her dancing fingertips. "From what they've told me, you're quite the studious little bee. You've the highest marks in your entire group. History, above all subjects, being your strongest interest. I was quite surprised to hear it. They've also mentioned that you've been getting into fights with this Bera fellow. Isn't he Bernardo Terranova's boy?"

Xolo's head drops in a hangdog manner. He protests under his breath. "Yeah . . . that's him. But none of what they say is true. I–I haven't been in any fights with him or anyone else. I–I swear it, my Queen."

"I've told you before, Xolo, you may call me Isabella. You forget, I'm more than just your Queen." Isabella reminds him with a small smile. "And I know all that playground gossip is nothing but lies. You would've been expected to take a swing at him for it to be considered a fight. I know you to be a gifted warrior, Xolo, so why do you allow yourself to take the beating?"

"I–I didn't want to fight him." Xolo's answer is timid. "I was afraid of hurting him."

"He didn't seem all too afraid of hurting you." Isabella tilts his head back up with a single hand. Her touch is gentle and caring. She calls out to his gaze. "Look at me. I know you well enough, my brave warrior. You're a noble and gentle spirit. This path will devour you. A warrior who refuses to fight. Strange. Why would you ever choose the life of a warrior then? What do you hope to find in the end?"

"I want to be a hero," Xolo answers with naivety. "Just like you and the others who fought in the war."

Isabella gives him an empty smile. "Then your suffering shall be greater." She turns towards her reflection over the water. Her eyes swell with pain and her voice grows heavy with sadness. "They'll write poems and songs about you. But they'll never mention the pain of your choices. How can they? When they can't even begin to touch your tears. It's easy to look upon your scars with praise and romanticize the horrors of your crusade. But their words can never reflect the fear that haunts you. The fear of overlooking your tomorrows, waiting on the day when your bygone sins eclipse over them in retribution."

She turns back to Xolo. Her gaze is yearning, lost and alone. Xolo doesn't know what to say, and blinks, confused.

Isabella lets off an uneasy laugh. "My brave warrior—a hero's quest is nothing more than a fool's journey."

The water ripples, and spots of white snow consume his vision.

April 13, 2222, 3:45 a.m.

The mosaic fades into memory, and he returns to the present.

Xolo stands with a hard glare piercing the impenetrable darkness before him. For a moment, he was that frightened, weak boy from his memories. His eyes quiver with sorrow, and tears gloss over them. The *macuahuitl* breaks down to its dormant obsidian mold and, for the first time, Xolo takes notice of the snow. He wipes off the string of blood that trickles down from his nose and trots back to the accursed town.

Rubí tucks in Balam for the night and crawls out of hiding once Xolo shrinks away back into Berumbo. Though they shared no words together, she felt his sorrow. She thinks about that very feeling as she makes her own way back to Berumbo's town square. She stops by the fountain and is ashamed for what she has done. Xolo sought solitude to contemplate on whatever phantoms troubled his sleep, and she robbed him of that. She is a thief and felt guilty for the crime. Now it is she who is contemplative.

"Whatever were you thinking about, my brave warrior?" Rubí wonders well past the comfort of her dreams and into the years to come.

CHAPTER 4
THE TOWER OF ICE

April 13, 2222, 6:05 a.m.

The sun rolls up from the eastern mountain range.

In Berumbo, this makes no difference. Smoky, grey clouds snuff out the celestial giant in a cataract blanket, and though four or five homes flicker with lights, Berumbo's snow-laden cobblestone roads remain silent. The sole sound heard on this decisive morning is the whisper of a spectral zephyr. Berumbo's day of judgment is finally here, and its salvation comes at a hefty price paid in stacks of gold and silver and jars of honey.

Santa Ana has been awake since the early hour of 5:00 a.m. He busies himself cleaning the barrels of his pistols and custom made four-barrel rifle. The Lucky Kid takes in a long drag on the cigarette wedged between his lips and exhales a thick contrail from his flared nostrils. Santa Ana squints at the rising, swirling smoke. He is left rattled by the forming shape—a skull grins at him with playful dread.

"Is that you, Death? You've come here to mock me, have you?" Santa Ana hisses with abject defiance. "Fuck off, you eunuch, maggot muncher. My soul is slave to your magnanimity, yes, but not today. I ain't leaving with you just yet. Not 'til I've reached my promised paradise here on this earth."

Santa Ana takes in another drag from his cigarette with a shaky hand. He carries on with cleaning his guns, letting the phantom claw that scratches down his spine go numb.

Sweat and drool drenches Savani's lower jaw. He growls like a rabid dog while nailing his thorn-studded brass knuckles against the bedroom wall. Matchwood pecks his face, and hot breath fumes from his clenched maw. The lust for Rubí that once flowed throughout his veins now burns cold with rage. Savani no longer thirsts for her nectars, not after the humiliation he suffered the previous night. His wrist still aches bruised from the mutant's grip. A primal bloodthirst consumes Savani. His rasped fangs pierce his lower lip and a thin stream of blood washes over his frizzled chin.

"Stupid, stupid little whore. I'll tear you in half at the legs, fucking little cunt." Savani licks the blood off his lips. "I'll make him watch, your daddy, make him watch his little girl bleed dead. Then, when his tears run dry, I'll cave in his skull. And the freak, I—I'll . . ."

Savani's voice fails. He knows Xolo will kill him with ease. His bravado fades, overcast with fear of a mere boy. The humiliation stings him in the gut. Savani caresses his pained wrist. The mutant's palm is burned over his thick hide in a dark bruise. Then, the drum of a familiar voice devolves him into a frightened, sobbing little boy.

"You're no boy of mine. You're not even a boy," the voice growls. *"You're a filthy and unruly flea ridden mongrel that's been pissing around the rugs and furnishings. Well, I'll have none of that now, not in this house, no sir. What do we do with unruly mongrels? I'll tell you, boy. We whip 'em 'til their skin is flayed clean off their backs and yours, my boy, shall go soft and wet. Not a whimper, do*

you hear me? Or else it'll be more lashings for you, yes indeed."

The crack of a distant whip over flesh deafens Savani's ears. He falls to his knees, and he cups his ears with shaky palms. Savani pleads to the distant voice, "Please, no more. No more, daddy. I'll be good. I'll be good."—he sobs.

Hot water cascades from the small faucet. The washroom is enveloped in a thin mist of steam. Xolo dips both hands into the water pooled in the sink. He cups a handful of the hot water and splashes it over his scarred face. He leans over the marble sink. The coldness pressed against his hands; it clashes with the warm droplets of water that drip from his chin into the waiting basin.

Sleep is a commodity Xolo hasn't been able to afford for many nights. After his late-night *danza de los diablos*, he returned to Room 9 and stood by the window. His empty vigilance ended after a few minutes. Rubí scurried past his view on her way back home, and it sparked his curiosity. He had figured the girl would have locked herself in her bedroom after the dishonorable incident with Savani at the barn. He never dwells past simple curiosity to question Rubí's lunar activities, nor does he sleep that night.

Xolo wipes the steam off the mirror. The streaks from his brushing fingers crack a gleam of his wearied reflection. His eyes flutter, longing for sleep, but he refuses to shut them for more than a wink. He splashes more hot water over his face and that is when Isabella's voice invokes him once again.

"What would you like me to say about your mother, Xolo? There is no fiction I can thread that won't unweave at the slightest of scrutiny." Isabella sighs and shakes her head in defeat, he recalls.

"I shan't torment you, not with the dark consequences your birth wrought upon her. She is gone . . . and you are here. You must understand, my brave warrior, this is what she wanted— for you to exist . . . but I fear it's not enough for you." Isabella's distant voice unsettles Xolo. It crept up on him from the unknown recesses of memory without being beckoned.

"We—um—I knew so very little about her outside of her being a human loyal to my sovereign claim. She scouted the battlefronts as a medic and her surname, Guevara, was the only thing

inscribed on her dog tag. At the time of your birth, you were discovered in a cave and a Xoloitzcuintli, the sacred dog of the underworld, kept you safe while your mother laid a corpse." Xolo gasps.

"*It was only fitting that you should bear the name Xolo to honor your guardian. You emerged from a strange oneness—a womb and a tomb. A strange oneness that burdens you with great expectations.*"

He can sense it, the darkness that bedevils Berumbo claws into the depths of his liquid soul, and he understands now—they might not survive this bounty. It makes no difference to him. He is not afraid to die.

An angry knock sounds at the door.

"You better be up, kid!" Santa Ana yells from behind it. "Hurry it up in there. We got a job to do!"

Xolo dries his face with the towelette. He grabs the sliver of obsidian and storms out of the room. The hunt is about to begin.

"Hiya!" Esteban whips the lead line, and the oxen let off a bellow. The carriage tugs sideways, lurching toward Berumbo's main road.

Salvatore and Osvaldo watch their only salvation leave from under the archway. But the men are not unaccompanied. Paciencia and Rubí are there as well. The girl is clasped to Paciencia by the hand. The carriage rolls past them, and Paciencia gives Xolo a small bow. Such a courtesy between warriors will ignite a fiery argument with Osvaldo, and he will spend the night at the barn with the oxen thereafter. Rubí breaks free from her godmother's grip and takes a few steps away from her. She taps her fingers, and waves goodbye to the mutant alone, quite bashful.

Xolo waves back, confused. A mutant seldom savors anything but revulsion from the artisans who shaped them.

Their trip is beset with snow and potholes, and the stubborn beasts fight Esteban's lead with every shrinking mile toward the accursed subterranean tower. Nonetheless, the oxen's instincts are quashed, and the carriage strolls through the town cemetery. Esteban maneuvers them around the tombstones and down the artificial road chiseled onto the mountain's rocky slope. The road hovers above the crashing tide below like a thin thread, and the oxen trudge at a slower pace.

"Homemade rum that'll burn a hole right through your gut, I promise you." Esteban chugs on the flask before passing it to Santa Ana, who sits beside him. "Yessir. Feel that sting, chewing the rim of your throat. Old family recipe, brewed it meself a few nights yonder."

"Not bad for a piss town yokel, if I do say so." Santa Ana cringes. "Goddamn! This fucking acid is going to keep me alive well after death."

"Ain't easy for me to hurl out what I'm about to say, but I admire all youse grit. I ain't got the nards to go back inside that cave, tower, or whatever meself." Esteban snorts. He grabs the flask back from Santa Ana and takes another swig. "So, I'm going to share with you the ugly truth about that thing you'll be trying to slay. That thing in there is no monster. I stared dead into its blood eyes that night of the massacre. They burned like hellfire, and they raped the sanctity of my soul. I felt it, something piercing my brain, digging, hungry to unearth my sins. Blessed be God, my sins never strayed far from the bottle. Monsters don't follow you out of your nightmares, boys. You're all going to die in there. Ain't any of you afraid of that?"

"No." Santa Ana's tone is blunt. "Don't think of us like little lambs. We answer to no shepherd. But neither are we wolves. I'd argue we're more like defiant little lemmings."

"Lemmings?" Esteban chortles. "Don't them vermin commit mass suicide by jumping off cliffs?"

"An urban myth concocted by cowards and cunts." Santa Ana flicks a match and lights a cigarette. After a short drag, he continues. "Lemming mass suicides are a migratory impulse. But take heed of the myth, chum. It illustrates the admirable quality of the lemming. Little fuckers aren't afraid to die. Crazy little nut sacks got bigger balls than the cunts who hired us for this job. You understand? Little rodent doesn't run from Death, it dives right into it and so do we."

"Sheep live longer than lemmings, chum." Esteban scoffs. "You do your thing and live life at the coin toss. Fifty-fifty chance we'll quaff more of this here rum again. But I ain't up for seducing Death's kiss. No siree. I plan to live a long and slothful life, pumping the gut with booze and grub while suckling on the breasts of cheap city whores," he burps.

"Disgusting." Savani snorts. He and Xolo

sit in the back of the carriage. Their eyes locked in a bitter tug-of-war. "Does it make you sick, boy? Catering murder and death to these spineless, eunuch cowards. Sure, it does. You're a warrior of Genesis. You've got a code of honor to uphold. Huh. But you ain't got no honor, boy. That's why you're here with us," Savani taunts with a sneer.

He continues. "They think themselves men when they can't even stomach bathing their own hands in blood and guts. We claim their sins for a price and beckon the inferno to swallow us. Not your ordinary nine-to-five job, is it? But fuck it, we're good at it and damnation is worth every penny—and in the end, they still think themselves better men than us. They call us vermin and villains—damnable bastards. It makes them feel like saints. Fucking hypocrites. At least we don't pretend to be otherwise."

Xolo says nothing. He turns away, bored.

"You hate me, don't you, boy?" Savani continues to taunt Xolo. He wants to inflame the mutant's slumbering rage. He is still sour from the humiliation forced onto him. "Oh, yes, you do. Those eyes of yours, I can see the murderous intent swirling behind them. You want to slice my throat, boy? What are you waiting for?

Go on, do it. Come now, I want you to try and gut me."

Xolo turns to Savani. His voice is tepid and low. "I don't hate you, Savani. You're not worth the effort, slight as it may be. The sight of a cockroach causes me some mild irritation, but when it comes to you, I am left quite unmoved. I wouldn't even bother stomping the piece of shit you call a face with the heel of my boot."

Savani's fists clench white around the brass knuckles. The bait is almost too attractive for him to ignore. "Heh. You ain't fooling me, boy." Savani hisses. "You should've turned a blind eye back at the barn and let me have the girl. I would've wooed her first, whispered flowers into her milky ears . . . heh, I can imagine it, licking that neck of hers, soft like apricot. Once the job's done, I'll be coming back for her, and it'll be ugly. I'll jab my cock so deep and up inside of her that she'll hear every torn muscle and fractured bone. Blood won't just drip from between her legs, but her eyes too, and you'll be the one to blame for it."

"It'd be better if you turn around and never look back at this place, Savani. It'd be unwise if you did otherwise." Xolo replies. His glower narrows into daggers. "Touch that girl, even in thought, and you'll gag on your own cock. That, I promise you."

"Huh. Oh please, don't play the noble hero with me, boy. We both know what you are," Savani snarls with a smirk. "*El Bastardo de Génesis*—that's what you are. You think you can protect the girl? Just like you protected that bitch, Isabella? You're nothing but a worthless cur—"

Savani gasps with a sharp breath. His neck contorts inward, and he claws the air for a whiff of oxygen—not even a scream erupts out from his hogtied neck. His right arm trembles, snared at the wrist by an invisible paranormal clutch. Savani's right hand's grip tightens around the thorn-studded brass knuckle, and it begins to maneuver up towards his throat. The thorn's tip nips his neck, and Savani's eyes bulge in protest. A single bead of sweat then trickles down his brow when the thorn's tip pokes at his jugular.

Savani realized a little too late the bold, yet stupid thing he had just said. He is now under Xolo's mercy.

"Don't you ever defile her name with your breath again, Savani." Xolo warns the paralyzed Savani. He disgusts himself. For a warrior of Genesis to use their preternatural gifts in such a perverse display of power is deplorable and dishonorable. But Savani spat out her name, Isabella, and Xolo couldn't let such disrespect go unpunished.

Xolo takes a sidelong look at the carriage's driver's box. Santa Ana and Esteban are none the wiser to what is happening behind their backs. His eyes are locked with Savani's again. Xolo makes his threat heard. "I could kill you this instant, Savani. But then Santa Ana might try to avenge you. Unlike you, though, he's smart enough to be afraid of me. I can see it in your eyes, behind all that scowl and bark, you're nothing but a coward. I'm not afraid to die, Savani, are you?"

Xolo then frees Savani from the invisible chokehold and allows him to fling forward with a sharp gasp. Xolo wipes the string of blood that flows from his nostrils and flings it out toward the moving road with revulsion. Xolo lost control of the sleeping rage and betrayed his honor by tormenting a maggot like Savani. He hangs his head in shame.

"You—You better . . . watch your back . . . when we're inside that tower . . . boy," Savani gasps. He gulps a second wind. "That thing in there . . . won't be the only one hunting you from behind the shadows."

Xolo ignores Savani's empty threat. He stares at his shaky palms and questions the path his decisions have led him down. He has grown weary from experiencing so much death. "*Will it ever end . . . will my penance ever end, my Queen?*" he wonders in quietude.

"Hiya!" Esteban tugs the lead line. The oxen bring the carriage to a lurching stop. They have reached the western coastline but are still a few meters away from the mysterious cave. Esteban maneuvers the oxen to a hitching post set near the road. The coachman jumps off without a word to Santa Ana or the other two bounty killers and ties the oxen to the post.

"Why are we stopping here?" Santa Ana asks. He jumps off the driver's box, rifle in hand. "We're nowhere near the cave."

"Look again, chum. Cave's just a mile yonder." Esteban points north toward the cave. "I got you gents as far as I can. The oxen are too spooked and won't budge another inch. You'll have to make ways on foot from here while I set up camp."

"The oxen won't budge, or are you too afraid to get any closer?" Santa Ana asks.

"Makes no difference what I say. You're still marching on foot." Esteban huffs. He starts to set up camp. "I'm not like you fearless lemmings. I'm scared down to the white of my bones. That cave there is cursed, and certain death awaits anyone foolish enough to walk inside of it. I'm content with living the life of a coward, so long as I get a lease on life for a bit longer."

Santa Ana scoffs with disgust. He hawks and spits a phlegm bomb over Esteban's toes. The coachman laughs it off.

"Bums off the cart, boys," Santa Ana calls to Xolo and Savani. "We're going to take a stroll down the beach and make our way to the cave on foot from here on out." He turns to Esteban. "If we're not back within two hours past high noon, consider us and your piss stain of a town dead."

Xolo and Savani jump off the carriage, and the trio of bounty killers trek down the beach towards the cave's howling mouth.

Xolo stops short behind the other men and blinks, confused. He thought he spotted two glinting red dots behind the cave's shadows spying on them. But then, as he blinks for a second time, they are gone.

"I forgot to mention," Esteban yells back at them. "May God be with you all."

"Fuck off!" Savani barks back.

The high tide makes it difficult for the bounty killers to hop along the slippery, algae-ridden rocks. The tiresome exercise takes Xolo back home, back to Genesis' Ayotl Rock Coast, where the ancient tortoises mated and roamed. He remembers admiring the tortoises' wizened, sunbeaten faces. Though slow, Xolo understood these creatures to be Death's greatest adversary—how else then, did they live for hundreds of years? Listening to their quiet wisdom always silenced his troubles. But that is a distant memory belonging to a stranger, and there are no tortoises here on this forsaken coastline to silence his torment.

The bounty killers cement their feet over the moist sand and enter the cave.

Santa Ana and Savani move a few paces ahead while Xolo lags. He examines the cave's walls. Streaks of blood and claw marks are spread across it like welts over skin. Xolo's fingers feather along the claw marks. The scratches are deep and powerful. His eyes pan to the sandy ground, and Xolo discovers a trail of fresh footprints. The Shark Monster is wise to their arrival.

"What're you looking at over there, kid?" Santa Ana asks.

"There are claw marks on the walls and footprints on the sand." Xolo saunters towards his partners. "The prints are small and light. Whatever this thing is, it's no bigger than a child and of a willowy build. The claw marks worry me, though. They're deep. It cut right through stone as if it were paper."

"Petite and strong. Salvatore said this thing shaved his team of twenty strong men down to a cowering four in mere minutes." Santa Ana straps the four-barrel rifle over his back and regards the surrounding darkness with caution. "Mind the echoes gents and don't forget, we're not alone."

The stench of rotting flesh creeps inside their nostrils long before they reach the corpse-strewn campsite. It is an unholy sight of severed limbs and guts frozen in the early stages of putrefaction. Though each bounty killer has experienced and unleashed his own share of horrors, none has ever seen such a perverse portrait of pure hate. For the first time in their seventeen-month long partnership, the three are in unanimous agreement.

They are in fear of the shadows.

"What the fuck is this thing?" Santa Ana grabs the crucifix wrapped around his neck and kisses it. He then crosses himself with a shaky hand. "Gather whatever limps you can find, pile them up, and we'll give these half-corpses a proper sendoff."

"They're all eaten up . . ." Savani's voice dims to a whisper. "Just like my brother's victims." Savani slumps over and retches up white bile.

An arm, a leg and, at times, a discarded liver, or severed head litter the ground. Not one corpse is found whole. The Shark Monster's feast after the slaughter was glorious.

Xolo discovers several shattered and mar-rowless bones near a small ridge. He tosses the bones in with the rest of the Shark Monster's discarded leftovers and heads back to the tent set up just over the same ridge.

The tent is intact at most. Xolo rips the cloth off by the pegs, should the Shark Monster be hiding behind it. The tent is empty, except for the few personal effects of whoever occupied it before the massacre.

A framed photograph snatches his eye. The glass is shattered, but the burnt sienna photograph behind it remains untouched from the chaos that razed the camp. A family is preserved inside its cropped borders. Xolo recognizes the man. Salvatore stands cradling an eight-year-old Rubí in his arms. The little girl has her arms wrapped around his neck. To his left is a beautiful, unsmiling woman, who Xolo gathers is Salvatore's grief-stricken wife. A hard truth to believe they are married. Their unhappiness is palpable with their hands touching at the fingertips alone. A single smile unbalances the perfect portrait of misery, and it comes from the little boy, younger than Rubí, clasped against the woman. Xolo knows this boy is none other than Salvatore's lost child, Santiago. He wonders what pieces of the boy are left behind to cremate or if the Shark Monster swallowed him whole.

Xolo pulls the photograph out of the frame and pockets it. A leather-bound journal is the next item to attract his attention. He thumbs through the penned pages and discovers it belonged to Salvatore. The pages are filled with detailed catalogues of the excavated artifacts and notes on the glyphs engraved over the walls.

He continues to sift through Salvatore's infinite scrawl and stops on one entry—an incomplete map of the subterranean tower. The map reveals that Salvatore's team only managed to survey three of the tower's unfathomable sublevels.

He reads further through the crisp pages.

September 10, 2221

Today we crept deeper into the labyrinthine tunnels and uncovered a series of passageways leading into catacombs and subterranean courtyards with undisclosed functions. Crystals with natural, white fluorescence illuminated these buried courtyards. The torches were hardly necessary except when marking our path while maneuvering through the passageways' abysmal, shadowy depths. This structure must sink hundreds, if not thousands, of leagues underneath the earth—we've explored a scant three sublevels with no known bottom in sight as of this entry.

My men were already overtired and hungry when we arrived at the third subterranean courtyard, so it was an easy bargain convincing them to grant me a short ten minutes to record our meager findings. I regret that "Courtyard 3" engendered nothing of great archeological value, just an unexceptional mask of basalt stone. Then again, perhaps it would be a tad remiss of me if I didn't mention the erratic recesses on the stone walls and the toppled tower over the pond that paint Courtyard 3 as an old theater of war. The oddest thing though are the paw prints speckled throughout the mud . . . the paw prints are of a small dog that walked a few steps around on its hind legs, almost like a man, before sprinting away on all fours.

Courtyard 3's glyphs are consistent with the rest. The most pronounced symbol is that of a "Shark Monster" with crossed bands and a dorsal fin on its back, and a split tail. This place—this tower—conceals many dark secrets I intend to exploit!

A weird theory crosses my mind. There are rumors of an existing tower in Genesis with a similar nebulous birth to this one. The mutants, those blasphemous perversions of the clay, have long horded its secrets and splendors, and they've no love for the artisans who shaped them. To parley an excavation at their tower is pointless, and my theory will remain a lingering question without an answer—is it possible for these two towers to be twins?

"Twins?" Xolo gasps. His eyes bulge with

shock. Never did he consider a connection between this strange structure and the one that erupted from Genesis' soil during its civil war.

"Is that the last of the limbs?" Santa Ana's voice echoes, and Xolo follows it.

"Don't see how it makes any difference if we missed a piece or two." Savani tosses a severed head into the heap of half-corpses. "We were hired to sever heads, not pick 'em and smoke 'em up."

"Yeah, I hear you, Savani. But when it comes to the dead, there's no price for decency." Santa Ana douses the half-corpses with a kerosine can he found. He catches Xolo walking back with the journal in his hand. "What do you have there, kid?"

"A journal with a partial map of this tower." Xolo continues to thumb through the pages. He stops on a rough pencil sketch of the basalt stone mask. A shakier hand drew it and marked it with a red dot above the brow area. The image unnerves him. Salvatore was right to suspect his people of hording splendors, much like the sliver of obsidian strapped to his thigh. He wonders what strange power lays dormant within this stone mask.

"So, turns out Salvatore wasn't exaggerating.

This place doesn't make a lick of sense. All right, kid, light it up," Santa Ana orders.

Xolo reaches to the obsidian knife strapped behind his belt—the *tecpatl*—and scratches it against a rock. The issuing sparks ignite the funerary pyre.

Santa Ana then dips a stick into the dancing flames to light a torch. "The world's gone mad. Is there anything in that journal that might give us an edge against this thing?"

"No." Xolo replies with a blank stare. He closes the journal and pockets it along with the photograph. He stares into the fire, into the severed head's dead, white glare. The flames swallow it, peeling away the flesh to reveal a blackened, grinning skull.

"All right, we're done here. Let's go kill this fucker," Santa Ana growls.

The bounty killers follow Salvatore's found map into the tower's second sublevel. Santa Ana swerves the torch around, but the flame is unable to conquer the otherworldly shadows or ward off the cold constriction of this house, this Tower of Ice. Their hunt reaches a standstill. The embers from the torch crackle, and everything falls into silence.

"Can you hurry it up, kid?" Savani grits

his teeth. He can't stomach it—a man of his deplorable reputation, frightened of whatever may lurk in the shadows. But there is nothing out there in the shadows except for whatever he brought along with him inside his corrupted soul. "Fucking cockroaches are crawling up my asshole. They'll flood out of my mouth by the time you figure out the way."

"Shut the fuck up, Savani." Santa Ana barks. "The only thing that'll be crawling up your asshole are my pistols. Now shut the fuck up, before your pathetic mewling alerts our presence to the bloody thing we're trying to kill. So, which way is it going to be, kid?" he hovers the torch over Xolo's head.

"I'm working on it, okay? This guy's got a sloppy hand." Xolo turns over the pages, trying to map their trail in advance. "And if you both can just shut—"

Suddenly, an eldritch gust blows out the torch, their sole source of light.

"I see you," a gurgling cackle echoes from behind the shadows.

Santa Ana lights a flare. Its light spreads, revealing the Shark Monster among them.

The Shark Monster grins, showcasing its needled fangs with strings of blood seeping from the edge of its split lips. The bounty killers reach for their weapons, but the Shark Monster is faster—it punctures the stone floor beneath their feet with a single, bony fist.

The three killers fall into the gaping hole, and their gasps drown in the tower's unknown abyss.

CHAPTER 5

MONSTERS BORN OF MEN

Droplets of water pelt Savani's bald scalp. His head throbs with the bludgeoning force of an earthquake, and his vision strobes with bubbles of white light. He claws through the rubble of stone, desperate to wrap his hands around his lost thorn-studded brass knuckles. He has plummeted somewhere deeper into one of the tower's unexplored courtyards—a rock quarry—and his weapons slid off his palms during the fall. The surrounding darkness howls with dread, and Savani's damned soul ripples with paranoia, adrenaline flooding all through his thumping veins. It'd be a mortal blunder for anyone who is foe or friend—not that Savani ever cared for such useless tokens of vanity—to sneak up on him in such an overwrought state. He is a rabid beast wrestling with fear and is bound to bite anyone nearby with his buffed, gnashing fangs.

Clink—the sound of chirping metal makes Savani's heart thump like a herd of stampeding wildebeest. He has found his first brass knuckle.

Clink—now he has found his second and final brass knuckle. He wraps the vulgar weapons around his fingers and curls his palms into fists.

Clank!—he hammers the brass knuckle-fitted fists against each other. Sparks drizzle down over the puddles of water that soak his feet. He lets off a ravenous growl.

"Where are you?! Show yourself, coward!" Savani screams out. No response, except for the void's mocking echoes. His eyes prod the motionless boulders around him. He whispers to the shapeless shadows. "I know you're here. Your eyes betray you. I can feel their sick, licentious tickle over my skin. I am familiar with it, the hungry touch, all too well."

Savani's toes stumble on a discarded, rusted chain. He wraps it around his left arm, adding another weapon that'll aid in garroting the Shark Monster. He joggles the chain against the stones and challenges the Shark Monster. "There's no prey for you here today, monster! Just another predator. Come now, no more games. Let's find out who's the superior killer, shall we?"

A blur brushes behind Savani. The reckless bounty killer turns around, catching nothing more than the rippling footsteps over the water.

The Shark Monster toys with Savani's fragile forbearance. Its scraping claws and gurgling cackle continue to tease him from behind the shadowy veil.

"Don't toy with me, monster!" Savani growls. "I won't stand here and be ridiculed, you hear me?! Show yourself—coward! I'll chew off your jugular with my fangs and feast on your bones!"

Savani's threat stirs up another gurgling cackle from the Shark Monster and . . . the raw-boned creature slithers out from the shadows on all fours, hunched over like a dwarf gorilla, it's palms never touching the puddles of water. The Shark Monster's hands crawl about like spiders by the tips of its spear-like ebony claws.

They engage in an intimidation dance like two rabid dogs. They snarl, bare fangs, and drool, and death bleeds unabated from their mad eyes. Savani tightens his grip around the thorn-studded brass knuckles and the Shark Monster scrapes a claw over a boulder, issuing a cloud of dust.

"Come on!" Savani screams.

Man and monster charge toward one another like berserker bulls.

The Shark Monster leaps off its long legs and lunges upward in the air with a splash. It ricochets off the corralling boulders like a maddened toad, yet with the ease of a cricket. It lands behind Savani and slashes his back with an open, spade-like hand. Five streaks of torn flesh gush with warm blood, and Savani's painful yelps recede into the shadows.

The Shark Monster bulges and pounds his chest, and howls with blatant joy. The smell of fresh blood and the thrill of the carnage to come is sublime ecstasy to the beast. But the Shark Monster falls victim to its hubris for assuming Savani is nothing more than a mad dog without the bite to back up his bark. The Shark Monster takes another swing and attempts to spear Savani's back with its claws, unaware that Savani remains unfazed.

The Shark Monster's initial attack was but a mere scratch to the hardened killer.

Savani blocks the Shark Monster's second attack with his chain-strapped arm. The ebony claws grip the chain, snapping it, and pierce right through Savani's flesh with sinew and muscle shredded in a shower of blood. Savani winces but creases a jagged smile. He now has the Shark Monster right where he wants it—stupefied and within an intimate range.

"Dumb fuck." Savani hisses. He wraps a grip around the Shark Monster's neck. "I can stand to lose a few pints of blood, can you? Let's find out, shall we? I'm going to beat you down to a pool of red goo, fucker."

Savani's thorn-studded brass knuckled fist hammers down on the Shark Monster in an arching swing and the creature is knocked face down over the moist soil. The Shark Monster gags on its spewing blood for a few seconds. It then whips a pained look towards Savani—a huge slab of torn, bloodied flesh clings to the creature's left cheek. The pained look is fleeting, quickly creaking upside to a hideous grin that oozes with malicious satisfaction. Savani beats down on the Shark Monster's grin, ripping the flap of flesh off its face. Blood sprinkles every-where. The Shark Monster howls in agony.

Savani snickers. He pulls his arm and delivers a left hook uppercut. The Shark Monster is knocked off its feet and sent flying clear across the quarry.

"Hard to believe that a lanky motherfucker like you sliced and diced that entire flock of cocksuckers we grilled earlier." Savani boasts and chews off the Shark Monster's flesh bits that are caught on the studs of his brass knuckles. He then frowns, disappointed that the bounty's threat was nothing but a mere exaggeration from presumptuous, craven men. "You're just another dancing shadow made too big by the embers of superstition and gossip. I'm going to pop your gut now, monster, and make my way up to your heart. I'll eat it while it still beats and wash it down with your blood."

The Shark Monster growls and spews out blood. Its dislodged jaw jiggles, hanging limp by the sockets.

"Look at you, can't even grin no more."— Savani scoffs. He grabs the Shark Monster by its thin, oily seaweed hair and drags it across the quarry.

The Shark Monster spews a trail of blood from its gaping mouth, and its legs fall like noodles, scraping over the tower's stone. Savani pins the Shark Monster up against a jutting boulder and jabs its gut and ribcage with a barrage of thorned dukes. Its flesh is punctured without mercy, and blood is disgorged in gallons.

And the Shark Monster croaks a cackle.

Savani buries his armored fists into the Shark Monster's gut. He then raises his glance to admire the agony stitched across the creature's misshapen face. To his surprise, the Shark Monster readjusts its jaw back in place, stealing away Savani's grin and leaving him in utter confusion.

"That . . . tickled," the Shark Monster's throat rattles. It pierces its ebony claws around Savani's scalp like a prickly crown. Its reformed jaw creaks open, and a geyser of blood ejects from its gaping maw, wetting the paralyzed bounty killer in a crimson shower.

Savani is blinded and drowned under the crimson tint. He falls to his knees and vomits out mouthfuls of blood. He is left drenched, the blood still running from his frizzled beard.

Savani gasps for air and wipes the blood off his eyes. He blinks, unbelieving the sight forging before him. The tower's stone melts away, transmogrified to wooden panels.

Shadows bounce off a burning flame, and

they dance over the wood. Savani has been stolen away to a familiar cabin, where a familiar voice echoes his name.

●●●●

"Vicenzo, quick, grab the cloth. Hurry it up, before your father sees the mess," the soft voice of his mother, Theresa, trembles with fear. She runs to the sink and grabs the small cloth herself while Savani looks on, mouth agape. His mother has been dead for years and Savani is himself wedged somewhere between a memory and a nightmare.

Thump-thump, thump-thump—Savani's heartbeat drums.

Savani is the youngest child of Lucio Dadano and Theresa Savani. His older brother, Alphonse, had fled from their home at sixteen, abandoning the eight-year-old Savani to be prey to their father's rootless anger and sadism.

By the outskirts of Cuckoo Meadows lies their dirt road home, the town of Cantarranas. A small town much like Berumbo, Cantarranas' population is scarce, reclusive, and hidden behind a sheet of oak trees. Lucio works as a lumberjack, a job he enjoys. The swing of the axe and the maiming of the old earth is cathartic to his inherited pain, and it excites his unforgiving savagery. Theresa is the oily opposite of Lucio. She is a kind, loving mother to Savani, and though frail, her love anchors him to an acceptable sense of normalcy and decency. But Lucio is a monster who often bruises his wife's delicate frame over the most insignificant grievances or to sate the hate that dwells within him.

In a tint of red, Savani relives the blood-scented past.

One hot evening, Lucio's steak was a touch pink, just a few tones away from well cooked. But Lucio always has his steak well cooked. Any other way was unacceptable—unforgiveable. The madness behind his eyes churned into an unstoppable inferno. Young Savani is left mouth agape when his father grips Theresa by the hair and slams her face down on the steamy slab of cow.

She whimpers and witnesses her torture gleam off her frightened child's eyes. She bites down her lips and chokes on her sobs.

Theresa's silence shields Savani from Lucio's wrath.

"What's this shit?!" Lucio presses her face down harder on the steak. "Stupid, fat cow who can't even cook up a decent piece of cow. You expect me to swallow this piece of raw meat—is that what you want? I'll get sick, miss work, and lose out on an entire week's pay. Who's going to keep this family afloat then, you? Huh, you're nothing! You're a stupid bitch who can't even cook up a good piece of cow. No one's going to want to hire a stupid whore like you!"

Lucio's grip curls tighter in Theresa's hair. He jerks her up and smacks her in the right eye. Theresa flops down and bangs her head over the table. She staggers away across the floor on her palms. She continues to choke on her sobs, and she turns a swollen eye to her youngest son, Vicenzo. Her pouring tears pleaded for her son to mind his fears and quiet his hatred lest he provoke Lucio's demon heart.

"I could've choked on the first bite, you worthless whore." Lucio unstraps his leather belt. He yanks Theresa back up and bends her over on the dinner table. He nooses the belt around her neck and strangles her. "You think I enjoy doing this to you, huh? You're the only one to blame. You force my hand, Theresa—you always force me to perform these dirty, shameless husbandly duties. Poison me—you were trying to poison me! I'll choke you first, stupid, fat cow!"

A soft whimper creeps out of Savani's trembling lips. The boy clasps his mouth and shuns away from his father's needled glance.

"Don't you turn away, boy," Lucio snarls. "Look to me, boy."

Savani refuses to obey his father.

"I said—look—at me!" Lucio barks, and Savani obeys. "Look your mother in the eyes. Do you see it, boy? *She* enjoys this, not me, her. Fucking, sick nymphomaniac—she forces me to do this to her, boy—it is all her fault!"

The belt tightens around Theresa's neck. Purple bruises begin to stain her pale flesh. Her sobs pour out from the edges of her mouth in the shape of white foam. Savani never dares to disobey his father's command. He watches his mother's eyes roll back inside their sockets. He hears her breath dim, and darkness snatches her unconscious.

Thump-thump, thump-thump—Savani's heartbeat continues to drum.

"It'll be okay, Vinny," Theresa mumbles with a shaky voice. "One day, we'll run away, and—and we'll find your brother. Together, we'll run away from this shithole. We'll go somewhere far away, where your father won't ever find or hurt us again. Never again. Maybe we'll flee to Cuckoo Meadows. The Immortal Luchador will keep us safe there. Would you like that, Vinny, just you and me?"

Savani brushes his mother's silky auburn hair while she bathes.

Theresa's fingertips dance above the soapy tub water. She rubs her neck. The leather's burn still sizzles over her skin. She then lets out a deep sigh and pulls her frail form out of the tub. Her nude body is furbelowed with bruises, burns and scars.

Savani flinches with horror, and his hatred for his father grows a hundredfold. Some nights ago, Savani caught his father in their basement working on a pair of monstrosities—twin brass knuckles studded with thorns. He has since spent every night fantasizing about bludgeoning Lucio's face with them. But Theresa's love stifles Savani's dark metamorphosis into a monster born of Lucio's poisonous blood.

Another evening arrives. Theresa cooks a steak over the stove and Savani nibbles on a baked brownie. Neither suspects the inevitable, for this is the night the boy is to be consumed by his monstrous heritage and the night his mother's smile shall finally die.

Savani kicks the air from his chair. He is quite happy. He smiles at his mother, and nibbles on his brownie. He reaches for the glass of milk to wash off the crumbs speckled over his teeth. Savani's grip is weak, and the glass slips between his fingers. The glass falls to the wooden floor and explodes in a shower. There's nothing left except a harmless white puddle and shards of glass.

"Vinny, what did you—?" Theresa's hand trembles when the car headlights roll into the driveway. Lucio is home, and he will be in no mood for spilled milk. "Vicenzo, quick, grab the cloth. Hurry it up, before your father sees this mess."

Savani doesn't move. Fear paralyzes the boy. Lucio will beat him until he bleeds.

Theresa runs to the sink and grabs a small cloth. She plucks the broken glass off the floor and tosses the fragments inside a garbage bag with shaky hands. She then dabs the milk off the floor with the cloth, but . . .

It is too late.

The door creaks open, and Lucio enters the home. Both mother and son turn to one another, fear stitched across their faces. Savani turns a pleading glance to his father. Lucio sneers at the white puddle on the floor. Lucio's knuckles buckle with pent up rage. He saunters towards the kitchen and pulls out from the drawer the thorn-studded brass knuckles.

"Filthy, flea ridden little mongrel." Lucio brandishes the brass knuckles over his fists and hammers them together. The thorns' chime summons a flinch from Savani. "You've been pissing on the rugs and wood furnishings again, haven't you, boy? I've been too lenient here; this reckless bonhomie ends this instant! Come here now, mongrel. Time for another lesson in propriety. And not a whimper, do you hear? Or it'll be more lashings on your back. Yes, indeed."

"Lucio, please don't." Theresa leaps between her husband and son. She wraps her arms tight around his right wrist. "He's just a boy. A good boy, not like his brother. Please, it was an accident."

Lucio headbutts Theresa. Her nose shatters, and she falls to the floor in a rain of blood. Lucio then pounces on her with his entire weight like a boulder. He raises one armored fist and points to Savani with the other. "Not a blink, you unruly mongrel. This lesson necessitates a masochistic heart, if hesitant. Look your mother in the eyes, boy, and understand this: what happens next is all your fault."

"Vinny . . ." Theresa reaches out to her frightened son, desperate to caress his face one last time. But her touch will never reach him.

Lucio cleaves her skull with the thorn-studded brass knuckles, and her hand falls limp, cold and forever yearning.

Not a single tear trickles down Savani's face, nor does a whimper rasp in his throat. Fear of his father's wrath waylays his vengeance. His mother's blood spritzes across his face . . . it is still warm. He never disobeys his father. He maintains a monolithic stare while his father bludgeons his heart down to red goo.

Thump-thump, thump-thump—Savani's heartbeat slows to a soft drum.

Savani trembles. He has somehow devolved to that frightened child from his past. "I'm sorry, daddy. Please . . . no more. I'm sorry. I'll be good . . . I'll be good."—he whimpers.

The Shark Monster grins. It enjoys feasting

on Savani's trauma and moral decay. Savani remains snared in the dark, tactile illusion, unaware he cradles his bloodied, still beating heart in his hands. The Shark Monster's fun dulls, and he rakes Savani's gut with its ebony claws. Intestines and other organs gush out and splatter over the tower's stone.

Savani's death rattle echoes throughout the tower and drowns in the shadows.

Somewhere else, down the tower's unknown fathoms, both Xolo and Santa Ana hear Savani's fading death rattle. They are unmoved by his killing. Santa Ana flicks a match and lights a cigarette. Xolo thumbs through Salvatore's journal, fixated on the basalt stone mask. Two bounty killers remain, and they continue to trek down the tower's passageways, mindful of the embosoming shadows.

The cigarette butt fizzles when it bounces off the crystalline waters.

After circling blind around and down similar corners for countless minutes, Santa Ana finally breaches the labyrinthine passage-ways. He reaches one of the tower's infinite subterranean courtyards. This one is with a swelling crystal pond and a toppled stone pillar, flat at the courtyard's midway point. Crystal clusters sprout from the ashen sands and pour out a dim white light that floods the entire space. Santa Ana scans the massive enclosure and recognizes its design to be a gladiatorial arena. There are archways at the ground level and spectator seats rise in three tiers. He presses the crucifix wrapped around his neck with a sweaty palm, wary of the shadows that inhabit this coffin of stone and white light.

Santa Ana creeps toward the pond's rim and kneels to cup a handful of water. He washes off the dirt from his face with a gentle splash. The crystal, perspiring droplets rejuvenate the weary bounty killer. His forties are fleeting, and he has served as a paid attack dog for far too long. Santa Ana looks forward to the hunt's end. He will soon touch upon the fabled promises of absolution and salvation from immortal damnation.

Keeping an eye on his surroundings, he unstraps his four-barrel rifle, and slides four bullets in each barrel, and straps it back. He saunters around the stone pillar that's toppled flat over the pond with cocked pistols in each hand. Santa Ana is certain Savani is dead and he will not take any careless gambles with the dead silence. The shadows behind the archways are deceitful and traitorous, and Santa Ana knows the Shark Monster is a capable shadow swimmer.

Savani was more beast than man, and the Shark Monster slayed him with ease. Santa Ana has a perilous fight ahead of him.

Mutants, androids, and monsters born of men; Santa Ana has savored the impunity of killing each without mercy. But this Shark Monster is unique among the prey that has come before. This creature oozes with a supernatural air that predates mankind.

Santa Ana discovers a lump of harrowed dirt near the pillar. He believes it to be the work of the archaeological team that was slaughtered months ago. He bends on one knee to study the hole's rectangular impression with a running finger. They've unearthed a box. This much, he is certain. Though he is uncertain what secrets laid in it, he is certain it should've remained buried and hidden.

Bones snap and a gargling cackle draws Santa Ana's attention away from the hole. His eyes are pulled upward, toward the toppled stone pillar where the Shark Monster perches. The creature feasts on its fresh kill, Savani's corpse, and its ashen skin flakes like grating stone, clean of blood and punctures.

"Are you a devil of some kind?" Santa Ana questions with voiceless lips. He is dumbfounded that the Shark Monster snuck up on him without a sound.

Savani's lifeless, needled stare injects Santa Ana's veins with fear. But the bounty killer is staunch in his mission. He will endure this consuming fear and claim this final bounty at all costs. The Shark Monster twist Savani's head off from the rest of his corpse and tosses it Santa Ana's way.

Santa Ana is called the Lucky Kid for good reason. He cocks his pistols and fires two shots on instinct.

Pow! Pow!—one bullet bursts Savani's head to bone shrapnel and the second scrapes the Shark Monster's neck.

The Shark Monster is flung backward, off its feet. It writhes in petulant anger while blood gushes out from the bullet's scratch. Hot steam belches from the slits of its flattened nose, and it hisses at Santa Ana with baleful intent. The Shark Monster springs back on its feet and sinks its claws into Savani's corpse. It pries off the femur bone and hammers it against the stone pillar. The Shark Monster growls before leaping off the stone pillar with the bloodied bone set aloft like a club. In a sweeping, grey dust cloud, it lands across from Santa Ana and darts towards its predator, twirling the bone in the air like a maddened baboon.

Santa Ana cocks his pistols and pierces the cold air with a barrage of hot leaded points. A dust storm erupts from the firing barrels, blanketing the crystals' white light behind a thick, grey veil. The Lucky Kid fires round after round, feeling himself besieged by a jinx. His luck is failing him. The Shark Monster dodges every bullet. It twirls and bends its pliable body in impossible ways.

"What the fuck are you made of monster?" Santa Ana barks, eyes blinking with confusion. "Rubber? You—you ain't robbing me of my purgation creature! You die today, do you hear?! The Lucky Kid always gets his bounty!"

The bone club shaves the grey veil in a streak of blood. Santa Ana rolls away, not a second too soon, before the bone club clobbers his skull. A geyser of sand blinds Santa Ana but he pollutes the air with bullets. The thinning sand cloud soon reveals that the Shark Monster has dodged Santa Ana's blind assault. Its body has contorted in a serpentine zigzag.

The Shark Monster contorts its bones back into place with a needled grin. A third eye opens above its brow in a twirl, and the Shark Monster pounces on Santa Ana again with the bone club. But Santa Ana's reflexes are quick. The bone club hits the sand and Santa Ana pins it down with a singular boot. He cocks his pistols and squeezes the trigger, and the barrels roar with hot lead. The bone club shatters into bone shrapnel that speckles across Santa Ana's face. The Shark Monster's weapon is destroyed, and the Lucky Kid smirks. He aims the barrels at the Shark Monster's center eye, eager to blast away that hideous grin.

Pow! Pow!—the Lucky Kid misses the mark by a thin hair.

He is left mouth agape.

The Shark Monster arches its spine backward in a crunch to dodge the bullets. Its ebony claws touch the sand by the tip, and the Shark Monster scurries away behind the stone pillar like a spider in a bemused cackle.

Click. Click—Santa Ana's pistols have run dry of ammunition. He discards the pistols and tosses them to the side. Santa Ana isn't like Savani, who enjoyed toying with the bounty. The Lucky Kid is a professional. He keeps a firm grip on the fortunes that await him at the hunt's end. He unstraps the four-barrel rifle and chases after the Shark Monster, turning a sharp corner around the stone pillar.

The creature is nowhere in sight.

Everything falls still and dead silent. There are no visible tracks on the sand, no echoes nor ripples over the calm pond. There is nothing but Santa Ana's heavy, frigid breath.

"Where did you go, little mouse?" Santa Ana's boots sink into the sand. He tiptoes closer to the pond. He cocks the rifle. His eyes scan the empty silence, and his finger taps on the trigger. "Slithery motherfucker. I don't care what you are. I'm just here to kill you and collect my loot. One last kill, to earn my will and end my ill."

Santa Ana pierces the shadows with narrow slits. Nothing is there. He surveys the Shark Monster's old perch. Nothing. And he prods the shallow pond with the rifle's barrel. Nothing but ripples. The Shark Monster has vanished without a footprint or moan. Santa Ana turns his back to the pond, and, without a disturbing ripple, the Shark Monster emerges from the waters with a twisted grin across its gaunt face.

"Gotcha." Santa Ana swings back around and pushes the four-barrel rifle against the Shark Monster's chest.

The creature grabs hold of the weapon's barrel just before the ensuing blast. Santa Ana squeezes the trigger. A quadruple blast pierces the Shark Monster's ashen flesh, and Santa Ana is left in utter disbelief—the simmering, mortal wounds inflicted on the Shark Monster heal within seconds.

The Lucky Kid drops the rifle and reaches for his crucifix. He clutches it in deep prayer, something he hasn't done in years. "By the grace of Almighty God. Speak your name, devil—what are you?"

An ebony claw dives into Santa Ana's skull right between the eyes. The Shark Monster ensnares him in its web of illusions. A dark hand ripples Santa Ana's consciousness and the echoes of the past numb the poisonous sting.

The Shark Monster's dark gift exfoliates Santa

Ana's years like reptile skin, and he becomes a young man again.

Santa Ana is an anointed priest of the Church of the One Faith. He is spiritual leader and healer to the impoverished town of Boquillas. A handsome man, the women of his congregation are swooning with his oily voice and sultry eyes. But such pleasurable things of the flesh are of no interest to Santa Ana, a man who prides himself above base mortal appetites. He is a proud servant of the faith, and he shepherds his flock under the firm, immutable teachings of God with a fierce voice.

"O righteous Lord, we, your unworthy children, beseech you to deliver us from the evils conjured by the heretics who have claimed dominion over your Earthly kingdom. These heretics who believe themselves gods have stolen and corrupted your greatest miracle—the power of creation! Such petulance and hubris merits eternal damnation. The miracles they've spun wrought not beauty, but blasphemous monstrosities risen from the earth's ores and the sacred clay of our mold." Santa Ana has never given such a passionate sermon. Every word he speaks is like a plume of fire. His sermon will be renowned as one of the most daring by any servant of the One Faith. "Our world suffers, O Lord. Yet, we do not impugn your righteous vengeance against our transgressions. Our sins vindicate our suffering, and we are unworthy of your mercy, O Lord. But I, your humble servant pleads to you on bent knees and moist sweat for mercy upon your children. We are weak and we've allowed these heretics to lead us astray from your glory—smite us down now if you must, for salvation's sake! Best we return now to the ashes than continue to reap the damnation we've sown, for we live in a world of monsters born of men."

His congregation rises from their seats in uproarious applause and riotous hooting. Santa Ana raises his arms to the air. He reaches out to touch the foretold Heaven and embrace the womb of God. The sermon is a success, and its sparks further inflame the scintillating conflagration that threatens a sleeping world.

Santa Ana smiles, pleased with his work.

She stands behind the third row, gazing upon the idealistic young priest with lustful eyes. Her name is Anne Gotha, the restless wife of Mayor Dax Gotha. For the past three months, Anne has sought spiritual counsel from Father Santa Ana. Dax, the unfaithful swine, has made a mockery of their marriage for far too long now. Anne has grown weary of his frequent indulgences with the whores who infest the local brothel. Thoughts of the other women sour their scant moments of intimacy. Anne can never stop imagining their faces whenever Dax lies atop her, drunk, plowing them deeper inside of her with every thrust.

Santa Ana lent his shoulders to her tears and lonesome heart. He provided Anne with the pure love she thirsted. "Love is an ever-lasting mandate of our church, and what I do aligns with what the Lord would have commanded"—Santa Ana would often tell himself during their private meetings in his chambers. Yet, Santa Ana's naïve hyperbole does little to allay the shame that festers within him during his intimate sessions with the belle, Anne.

And it is this Luciferian hubris that eventually leads to Santa Ana's fall from grace.

During one afternoon of prayer, their hands curl in a firm embrace. Anne's silky, warm touch steams his breath. Santa Ana's resolve weakens, and his eyes grope Anne's sumptuous breasts. This is his first time tasting the vile wine of desire, and the hunger for carnal fruits erupts within him. His loins pulsate with lust, and his heart palpitates with passion.

Anne desires him as well.

"No!"—Santa Ana bolts up from his chair. "I cannot submit to you. We mustn't. Our vows chain us to certain unbreakable commitments by the neck—you to your husband and mine to the One Faith. These are unbreakable chains under God's laws. If we try to pull away, we'd only hang ourselves."

"What good are our vows when we are bound to lies?" Anne moves closer to Santa Ana. Her breasts push up against his chest and her cherry lips inch closer to his. "Our vows are nothing more than mere words. Such words paint ideal lies that strip us of what we are—human, imperfect but beautiful, just the same."

Anne presses her moist lips against Santa Ana's, and the young priest surrenders to base human desire. A quick breath too late, Santa Ana pulls Anne away and storms off, sickened by his transgression.

Later in the night, secluded behind his chambers in the church's basement, Santa Ana implements his penance for having forsaken the One Faith's vow of celibacy. His back cracks with every lash of the bullwhip. Every thrash over his flesh sharpens his desire for Anne. He cannot stop the outpour of licentious fantasies of him toiling her nether parts.

The next day, he delivers another fiery sermon. Once the tired performance ends, his congregation exits through the doors. The last stomping footsteps draw out the noise behind the shutting doors, and silence falls. Santa Ana and Anne are left alone. Their eyes lock, and the original sin inborn to all humans consumes them. They abandon their Godly vows. Man and woman run to one another and give in to their lust with suckling lips and groping hands.

But they remiss to acknowledge the stained-glass saints and marble angels whose petrified, watchful gaze judges them in idle silence.

They escape down to his private chambers.

Santa Ana and Anne's nude bodies wrestle with an amorous fire. For the first time in his young life, Santa Ana acts like a man unclouded from delusions of piety and damnation. Sweat trickles down their backs, their breaths run hot over their necks, further germinating their forbidden passion.

Anne's breasts heave and she lets out a pleasurable sigh. She whispers to him, "I love you."

Both scream at the climax of their forbidden

passion. Santa Ana whips his gaze upward to the sacrificial Holy Lamb mounted above his bed. Its soulless, divine eyes pierce his soul with scorn. He has embraced the original sin and condemned his soul to eternal damnation.

"What have I done?" The frightened priest mumbles. Santa Ana turns a downcast look to Anne's nude body. She is the Eve to his condemnation. He grimaces in horror, and hooks his hands around her elegant, glistening neck. "What—? What have I done? What have you made me do? You—you seduced me! You have stolen me away from the Lord's womb! Whore of Babylon, you shall burn—with me!"

Anne's pleasurable sighs sink to terrified gasps. She claws Santa Ana's chest and arms, tearing off strings of flesh, but she cannot break his chokehold. Her breasts succumb to the coldness of death in a muffled whimper.

Santa Ana's eyes quiver in shock. The Church of the One Faith will cover up this crime to protect its integrity, and they shall then excommunicate Santa Ana. Anne's dying breath seals these inevitable certainties. He reaches to the drawer next to his bed and pulls out the bullwhip. He remains seated atop Anne's lifeless body, nude.

Santa Ana implements his penance.

The whip cracks with tender love over his flesh. Blood soaks the leather, and joyful tears rain down from his eyes. A gratified, stiff grin creases his face. He continues to thrash the bull-whip over his flesh. His atonement is blissful.

Never does he suspect he drowns in a dark illusion.

The Shark Monster claws Santa Ana's back. Every bloodletting scratch broadens Santa Ana's grin, and blood spews out from between his clenched teeth. Santa Ana falls to his knees with arms raised up to the air. He reaches out to touch the foretold Heaven and embrace the womb of God.

The Shark Monster spears Santa Ana's back with its ebony claws and cleaves him in half from the waist up. The Lucky Kid lives up to his nickname—he is blessed with a painless death.

From the dark, depthless shadows, Xolo emerges from the third spectator tier. He holds

Salvatore's journal. The mutant followed the partial map and navigated through the labyrinthine passageways with ease. Pocketing the journal, he takes in a panoramic view of the massive courtyard. He discovers Santa Ana and Savani's mutilated corpses over the pond. He never blinks with pity. Their brutal deaths fall silent in his heart. Xolo never liked either man. Their partnership and his association with the Bounty Killers Guild are of mere convenience and self-interest.

Neither Santa Ana nor Savani has proper inheritors and the guild's rules are clear. Xolo alone will reap the bounty's reward in full. But the mutant seeks not riches set in gold, silver, or honey. What Xolo seeks is above empty material value.

He seeks redemption.

The air falls dead, and colder. Xolo can sense the Shark Monster is nearby, but he is unsure where it hides. He hovers an open palm next to the sliver of obsidian strapped to his right thigh. Xolo inches toward the spectator tier's edge. He sees nothing but feels an icy breath, rife with the stench of death, brush the back of his neck.

Xolo swings around and confronts the

Shark Monster's crooked grin. The creature's molten-blooded eyes and third, twirling eye above the brow, invite him to engage in *la danza de los diablos.*

CHAPTER 6
WARRIOR OF SHADOW AND JADE

From the very moment they stepped onto the coastline's sands, the scent of the bounty killers' warm blood crept inside the Shark Monster's nostrils. Their interloping stench disturbed its feast of common salmon caught from the nearby waters. But there was something different about this prey. An oddity walked beside them down the coastline. This oddity's stench caused the Shark Monster's nostril slits to flare—the stench was unlike any the Shark Monster had smelled before. The Shark Monster discarded its beggar meal and scurried through the labyrinthine passageways in great haste.

It reached the cave's mouth to take a small peek at the coastline.

The trio of bounty killers were a few meters away, marching steadfast towards his dark realm, unaware of the death wish their shuffling footsteps hauled along. The balding brute and cowboy reeked of common mortal foibles, but the third, a mere boy, was more underneath the skin.

This boy's strange stench piqued its curiosity, and the Shark Monster hared off back into the tower's abyss, back to its meal of raw salmon, where it waited with great patience for the prey—these pathetic, deluded fools who dared to presume themselves slayers of Death.

The funeral pyre's crackling embers obtruded into the Shark Monster's eardrums—the bounty killers have finally invaded its icebound realm. The Shark Monster swam among the shadows and stalked the quarreling killers. Unseen and unheard, the creature snuffed out their small fire, and then lunged out to split the bounty killers' small phalanx.

The Shark Monster's hunt had begun. The first to be slain was Savani, the weakest of the three. Shortly thereafter, it was Santa Ana. They were mere mortal men with sinful souls polluted with the decay of remorse—bothersome flies tangled all too easy by the gossamer threads of its dark gift. The Shark Monster savored toying with their wistful specters and culling them like pigs. But the boy, it would spare him for last. Somehow, the mortal oddity occluded himself from the reach of its dark gift.

"Strange . . ." the Shark Monster gargled with mouthfuls of meat and bone from Santa Ana's corpse.

Xolo's near impenetrable, unnatural essence makes him a real threat. The Shark Monster snickers with a horrid, bloodied grin. It will find great amusement in their imminent *danza de los diablos*.

The Shark Monster meets Xolo's stiff glare with a fang-baring snarl. A rancid breath sears Xolo's face and thin strings of drool pelt his defiant, unblinking glare. Mutant and monster are petrified with mutual shock, unknowing of what to make of the other's otherness. Xolo's righthand fingers quiver. He attempts to reach for the sliver of obsidian strapped to his thigh, but the Shark Monster is faster—it pushes him off his feet. The powerful blow sends Xolo flying across the courtyard and he lands on the shallow pond in a streaking splash.

Xolo is left punch-drunk but pushes his breathless self to regain composure. Again, the Shark Monster's lanky form shifts in agile speed. In the wake of a silent gust, the Shark Monster materializes by the pond in front of Xolo! Its crooked smile taunts him, goads him to engage in *la danza de los diablos*.

The young warrior arises, gnashing his teeth with palpable anger. The Shark Monster shifts its position again—behind the confounded mutant! Xolo reaches for the sliver of obsidian strapped to his right thigh. He summons the full totality of his preternatural gifts, and a wave of green energies transmutes it into the *macuahuitl* of black volcanic glass.

The prismatic blades studded all-round the *macuahuitl's* edges strobe with green light. *La danza de los diablos* begins with bestial fury!

Xolo's every swing from the *macuahuitl* is dodged with ease, and the Shark Monster bombards the spurned mutant with blurring claw slashes. Gashes across his face, chest and shoulders leak warm blood, but Xolo never weakens. He continues to swing the *macuahuitl*, and his face endures a shower of blood from every fresh gash. The Shark Monster pierces Xolo's stomach and scratches his right arm, weakening his clutch on the *macuahuitl*. Xolo has lost his weapon but is far from demoralized. His warrior's spirit remains defiant!

His hands curl into bone-knuckled fists and he assaults the creature with them. He lands several powerful dukes on the Shark Monster's chest. The blows furrow deep on its stony flesh like footprints over sand and their impact quakes the tower's very foundation.

The Shark Monster's legs stand firm against the sloshing pond water, unshaken from Xolo's hammering fists. It croaks a laugh and slaps Xolo across the face with its ebony claws. Xolo is flung backward but boomerangs around with an air shaving fist that flies straight at the Shark Monster's third, twirling eye. The Shark Monster blocks the blow with a clawed palm. The defensive parry erupts into a shockwave that splits apart the waters beneath their rooted feet. Xolo is locked hand to hand with the Shark Monster, and he blinks with confusion when he notices the third eye's subtle, worried twitch.

"Your stink . . . it's different from the other

two," the Shark Monster sniffs with salivating hunger. A bemused smile creaks across its ugly face. "Oh, those heathen and clever monkeys. How have they maimed and profaned the clay of their mold." The Shark Monster unhooks Xolo's fist and grabs him in a chokehold. It lifts him off his feet and tosses him across the courtyard. The Shark Monster lunges after Xolo and pins him against the tower's stone enclosure.

The Shark Monster has grown bored with its mute prey. It swings back a clawed hand, intent to gore out Xolo's heart and sate its immortal bloodlust. The ebony claw slides through the air but halts an inch away from Xolo's left eye. The Shark Monster winces with ire—it cannot push its claw further.

An invisible hand gripped its wrist!

The Shark Monster's glower leans in closer to meet the boy's eyes. "What . . . are . . . you?" The creature wheezes with repulsion.

Xolo tilts his head back. The creature's question has him further confused.

"Just how long has this fossil been buried?" Xolo ponders with a mute voice.

He snares the Shark Monster with another spectral grasp around the neck. Its shriek pierces the air like shattering ice, and both fall to the ground. Xolo summons the *macuahuitl* back to him with his gift and tosses the Shark Monster across the pond, crashing it against the stone pillar. He reverts the *macuahuitl* to the sliver of obsidian. He removes his bomber jacket and waits for the Shark Monster to make the next attack.

The Shark Monster spins in a childish tantrum on the sand. Its rage simmers to a venomous hiss aimed at Xolo.

"Come on!" the mutant goads with a waving hand.

It takes the bait! The Shark Monster pounds its fists against the toppled stone pillar and charges towards the mutant.

Xolo waits until the creature is a few paces closer to him. The Shark Monster lunges his way with a swinging ebony claw. Xolo slings the sliver of obsidian up in the air and somersaults behind it. He evades the Shark Monster's attack and grabs the sliver of obsidian midair.

Xolo lands behind the Shark Monster and reconstitutes the *macuahuitl*. The creature attempts another swinging claw attack, but Xolo dodges it and lops off the Shark Monster's right arm. Blood geysers out from the wound. The Shark Monster howls in agony and unleashes a berserker claw barrage at the mutant with its one remaining arm. Xolo grabs hold of the arm and twists it behind the Shark Monster—bone shatters with a loud crack. Xolo then snuffs the Shark Monster's pathetic howls by crushing its larynx with the *macuahuitl's* hilt. He then plunges the creature into the pond.

Xolo stands back and watches the Shark Monster choke on its own blood with icy disdain. The mutant is without pity or mercy; previous battles have wilted his compassion towards all foes. He cements the *macuahuitl* on the ashen sand and leaps at the Shark Monster. He locks its head around his arms. They tussle for a short minute before Xolo snaps its neck with a powerful twist.

The Shark Monster's lifeless body drops to the water in a gentle splash. Xolo gives in to exhaustion and falls to his knees. He is the lone survivor of this accursed bounty. Yet his heart remains empty, and such bittersweet serenity is short-lived. Snapping bones draw his attention to the Shark Monster's severed arm. It convulses in an epileptic fit before standing erect on its ebony claws. It then spiders away towards the Shark Monster's stiff corpse.

"You've got to be fucking kidding me . . ." Xolo mouths in utter disbelief.

Hot breath boils the waters, and the Shark Monster reawakens from its brief death. Its head dangles in a lopsided manner from its shattered neck. The severed arm sprouts vines of sinew and muscle that reattach themselves to the Shark Monster's bloodied wound, and it twists back into position. The Shark Monster cracks its neck back into place, and finishes mending itself.

"Hurrr . . ." the Shark Monster purrs with a needled grin. It shakes a disapproving finger at Xolo. "Tsk, tsk, tsk. Good, you're very good. But not good enough. Still nothing to say, eh, boy?" it utters with a throaty voice.

Xolo doesn't answer. He narrows his eyes and uproots the *macuahuitl*, ready for the second bout.

"You wear the prey's skin over your bones and meat, and even bleed red as they do." The Shark Monster saunters towards Xolo with dancing claws. "But the stench all about you is different, and your blood's taste is far saltier.

Underneath the skin, you're nothing like them. But their fingerprints are marked all over your being, down to the bone and blood. You're stronger, mightier than the prey . . . what are you?"

"Weird," Xolo takes a few paces back. His eyes flutter with strain. "I was about to ask you the same thing."

"Hurrah! The abomination can speak!" The Shark Monster howls. "But, tsk, tsk, it is most rude. I asked first, boy. I'm curious—will your meat give me an upset stomach? Oh, yes boy, you'll join the rest in death. I shall savor gnawing the meat off your bones the most."

"A warrior of Genesis fears nothing, monster, not even death." Xolo's eyes twitch. He resists the spade of the Shark Monster's dark gift over his mind. "My journey is one of strife and blood. I've long foresworn love and joy for the dead have no need for either. But today is not the day I shall die."

"A warrior, you say," the Shark Monster cracks its neck. It circles Xolo, with the third, twirling eye pinned on him. "You are unlike the other two. Your eyes gleam with honor, a fatal flaw for one sworn to a life celibate of love and joy. Why would you ever choose the life of a warrior? What do you hope to find in the end? Oh, there it is . . ." It drills a single claw against its skull with a twisted grin. A single string of blood trickles down its right cheek, ". . . to be a hero."

Xolo stumbles backward. The distant voices of ghosts invade his eardrums—voices he's long tried to bury in the past. He takes in several strenuous breaths and tightens his grip around the *macuahuitl's* hilt to a burn.

"Xolo . . ." the voices howl.

"You are a stubborn one, boy. Is it not tiresome to be brave for so long? The other two gave in to their penitent hearts with ease. Why not do the same? Give in boy, give in to your shame." The Shark Monster sniffs the air about Xolo with ire. "I don't want your fear, boy!" It hisses. "Why savor on the fleeting flavors of fears, when plaintive scars are ripe eternal for a delicious bloodletting feast?"

Xolo bares his clenched teeth at the Shark Monster with abject defiance.

"Very well, fear it is . . . for now." The Shark Monster growls. "I shall then teach you why men once feared the dark." It takes a few steps backward, and steals away the white light, sinking them in pitch darkness.

Xolo's *macuahuitl* strobes with green paranormal energies like a lonesome lantern lost amid the ocean of darkness. Xolo treks with heavy breaths, cautious to every plodding sound.

Then, the first of the ghosts beckons him from the darkness . . .

"Whatever happens today won't change a thing. Our curse is unbreakable, immutable . . . eternal. They will always fear us. They will always fear you . . . and we cannot blame or hate them for it, not when we embody their inevitable doom. Embrace their scorn and fear, brother, for we are harbingers of Death here to mete out their extinction."

SHRIEK!

The *macuahuitl* scrapes against the Shark Monster's ebony claws in a shower of green beads. Xolo falls on one knee and blood drips from a fresh wound scratched over his right ribcage. The Shark Monster descends back into the shadows with a fading silence.

"You think yourself brave, carrying on with this defiant posture . . . you're a fool, Xolo. I bear the same ugliness that haunts you—the monstrosity of our bloodline. And I can say this to you with certainty that your sacrifice is wasted on them. What have they ever given us besides an obscure existence? I say let these winding atrocities undo them. That way they'll never forget us or dare to question that we ever existed," the second ghost taunts him.

"Shut up!" Xolo screams. He swings the *macuahuitl* with blind fury. "Shut up! —Shut up! —Shut up!" he barks. "It's not them, it's not them . . . I know it's you, monster!"

The Shark Monster flashes between the *macuahuitl's* every blunting shave, and its ebony claws hack away at Xolo's meat with malicious glee.

Then . . . silence falls again.

Xolo's face is wet with droplets of blood and sweat. A haze of rage blurs his vision. The darkness sinks him deeper into the trenches of trauma, and the ghosts, their voices, recede back into the ephemeral shroud of memory. Xolo cannot ignore the shrinking echoes, not when they corrode his shield of fear down to rust. His grip on the *macuahuitl* weakens.

"Your fear wanes, usurped by an angry and contrite heart, good. You're fleeing . . ? Strange. You do not run away from man or Death . . . whatever do you hope to escape from poppet, if not the darkness that festers within your heart?" the Shark Monster calls out.

Xolo's resistance to the Shark Monster's dark gift weakens. He lowers the *macuahuitl* and allows the rotting breath of Death to mist the back of his neck.

"Every journey comes to an end . . . Xolo, my brave warrior, what do you hope to reach at the end of yours . . ?" Isabella beckons him.

He turns, and, in a great white flash of lightning, the Shark Monster snares him in its dark web of illusions.

●●●●

The Shark Monster's dark gift has swept Xolo away into a realm of black, volcanic glass. His knees buckle and he falls on his hands with a grave splash. A gasp escapes his mouth, and he rises on bent knees to the sight of his hands submerged in dark blood. The river of blood's wetness, even the stench of it, is nothing more than a touchable illusion, but an illusion all the same.

Xolo rises to his feet to confront the roaring tempest that lurks behind the dark reflection over the glasslike obsidian trench. His reflection—his shadow soul—meets Xolo with a crabwise glance. And those bulging, mad eyes imprisoned behind the obsidian trench, they flood with a golden fire.

"No . . ." he utters, unable to shun away from the grinning shadow soul.

SCREECH!

A claw scrapes over the volcanic glass.

Xolo cups his palms over his ears. And the shadow soul scurries off onto the undergloom of Xolo's soul, away from the snaking cracks.

"How . . ? This . . . this is not possible." The Shark Monster protests echo. "You are different from the other prey. You shield your soul from my dark gift. How can this be? What manner of abomination are you, boy?"

Xolo's eyes bulge open. He spins around, searching for the shadow soul . . . and he runs away.

SCREECH!

The Shark Monster's dark gift scrapes the volcanic glass a second time, and Xolo twirls through the obsidian trench, sprinting ahead of the sounds of shrieking glass.

"Open your broken and maimed soul to me, boy. Allow me to feast on the deliciousness of your sordid nightmares and imbibe on the squalid juices of your traumas," the Shark Monster roars.

SCREECH!

The Shark Monster's dark gift scrapes the volcanic glass a third time, and Xolo's splashing flight draws up.

"Yes . . . that's it. Run no more, poppet." The Shark Monster cackles with smug satisfaction. "Why do you run? Avow to me the specters that haunt you. You cannot repel my dark gift forever, boy, no more than you can bargain with Death. In the end, all things bow to us . . . Death is unconquerable, inescapable, much like the darkness blest upon your blasphemous race."

Xolo reaches a clean, impenetrable obsidian mirror. The shadow soul emerges behind its foggy essence with a horrid grin. Xolo takes two steps back. The shadow soul takes two steps forward and breaches its glass prison. A single bead of sweat trickles down Xolo's brow . . . he is unafraid but becomes consumed with hate when his eyes touch upon the warrior of shadow and jade.

"What . . . are . . . you, boy?" the Shark Monster asks.

"Stop this . . ." Xolo commands with gnashing teeth.

"They will rid themselves of the virus . . ." The Shark Monster parrots a damnable voice familiar to Xolo, ". . . vanquish the enemies who've threatened their posterity, and you may arise as my slayer, but do not fool yourself. They will bestow no leniency upon you. They will never forgive nor forget whose blood soaks your hands with a red death, and no matter what lies you embrace you can never purge yourself of the blood that runs through your veins. I am your curse, and you are theirs."

"Shut up." Xolo mutters. "Don't you dare—don't you invoke HIM!" he hisses with steaming hate.

The warrior of shadow and jade outstretches an arm. A crescent, scythe-like bone barb protrudes from the forearm. Xolo stands defiant before the warrior's burning golden glower.

"Stop it . . ." Xolo lets off a hoarse growl.

The warrior charges towards Xolo, bone scythe scratching the obsidian trench, and leaps off its legs into the shadowy skies.

"No . . ." Xolo begs with a trembling lip.

The warrior plunges his way.

Xolo cries out in anger, "NO!" He spears the warrior with a single bare fist.

CRASH!

The illusion shatters in a black explosion of volcanic glass under Xolo's catapulting fist.

The Shark Monster leaps backward and perches itself atop the toppled stone pillar.

"Come on!" It goads with a bone-rattling cackle.

Xolo whips his head sideways and spots the discarded *macuahuitl* two steps away. He rolls towards it and makes a mad dash towards the Shark Monster with the *macuahuitl* streaking the sand beneath his heavy steps.

The Shark Monster howls with abated breath. It leaps off the stone pillar to meet Xolo's swinging *macuahuitl* with its ebony claws.

SHRIEK!

Obsidian blade and ebony claw clash. But their second bout pivots a different way.

Xolo has the upper hand. His stern gaze boils with a blood wrath.

The Shark Monster struggles to dodge the *macuahuitl's* grating sweeps, losing a flock of its seaweed hair. Its bravado blunts, and the Shark Monster's claws shave at the berserk mutant's chest, arms, and legs in utter desperation. But the boy's wrath is unconquerable—unstoppable, and this dark emotion seeps out from Xolo's eyes in a golden strobe.

The strangeness bewilders the Shark Monster.

Xolo tosses the *macuahuitl* to the ground. He then resorts to bombarding the Shark Monster—an unarmed foe—with telekinetic blasts. It is a deplorable violation of Genesis' code of honor, a sinful act Xolo is remiss to repress while consumed with bloodlust. He shatters the Shark Monster's knees and legs at the bones. The wailing creature topples to the sand, but never touches it. The assaulting spectral grasp lifts the Shark Monster midair. Xolo raises an open palm. He roars like a hellbent beast, and his invisible hands contort, bend, and twist the Shark Monster's every bone and limb in unimaginable ways.

"What . . . are . . . you?" the Shark Monster barks with a bloody drool.

Xolo hears nothing.

The Shark Monster's screams drown under the sounds of broken bones and torn muscles.

Xolo swings his raised arm sideways, and the spectral grasp tosses the Shark Monster across the courtyard. He lunges after it and pins it against the toppled stone pillar. Xolo's strobing, golden eyes pierce the Shark Monster with hate. He presses the spectral grasp over its chest and begins to claw out its beating heart. The Shark Monster's chest bone and ribcage splinter. The carnage incites a furious scream from Xolo, and the Shark Monster howls in genuine agony.

Xolo's gaze drifts away from the Shark Monster. He catches his reflection in the pond and is horrified by his dishonorable actions. And the golden eyes that stare back at him quash the wrath which has blinded him. Xolo falls to his knees, loosening the Shark Monster from his spectral grasp.

He hunches over and his clawing hands rake over his skull. "No, never again, never again . . ." he utters, shaken.

"You couldn't do it . . . finish me off, eh, boy?" the Shark Monster mocks while its body snaps back into place. "Honor, bravery, pathetic foibles befitting fools. Weaknesses that gain you nothing except a swift death."

It raises a claw, ready to lop off the cradling mutant's head.

Salvatore's journal creeps into his mind, and Xolo recalls the rough pencil sketch of the basalt stone mask. A red dot of blood had been stained on the drawing just above the brow area. Throughout their battle, the Shark Monster shielded itself but once, when Xolo attacked its third eye. The red dot is its third eye. Salvatore had said the Shark Monster was killable—the third eye must be its sole vulnerable spot.

Xolo reaches for the obsidian knife strapped behind his belt—the *tecpatl*—and jumps back up on his feet. He grabs the stunned Shark Monster around the neck and digs the obsidian knife through the third, twirling eye.

The Shark Monster screams and twitches in agony.

Xolo whips around and elbows the obsidian knife, digging it deeper through its skull. The Shark Monster's entire being ripples with unknown dark magicks that quake the tower's foundation. The magicks erupt, and Xolo is sent flying back, clear across the subterranean courtyard.

The Shark Monster bellows and writhes in

fits of agony over the sand. Its stonelike skin thins into flakes of ash. It daggers Xolo with a single, shaky claw.

"What . . . are . . . you, boy? I shall tell you . . . you are a creature of the shadows, born to bear the great burden of my tribesmen— forever scorned, doomed to eternal aloneness, for we offer the one, true magnanimity all creatures fear . . . death . . . hurr . . ." the Shark Monster croaks a final taunt.

Its face cracks like eggshell and the Shark Monster collapses on all fours. Its body shrinks to that of a child, and its death purr fades to a mewl.

Xolo stands on his feet again but remains back. He smears off the blood trickling from his nostrils and cocks a quizzical look. The Shark Monster is slain, this much he is certain. Yet, its final death has birthed some strange life.

The boy grunts. He struggles to stand on rattling feet.

Xolo gasps with bulging eyes. He knows this boy from the photograph. This boy is Salvatore's missing son—Santiago.

"Daddy, daddy . . . I–I'm scared . . ." Santiago's whimpers fall to a gag. He goes stiff and blood spews from his mouth.

Xolo watches with horror while Santiago's body erupts from every wound it suffered under the Shark Monster's possession. Savani's needled jabs and Santa Ana's gunshots gush fresh with blood. Santiago's right arm lops off in a string of snapping sinew and muscle, and the gashing wound above his brow sweats with red beads of blood. Santiago collapses to the ashen sands, bloodied, broken, and dead.

Xolo rushes beside Santiago's motionless corpse and kneels to cradle him in his arms. The boy's blood seeps between his fingers. The warm wetness frightens him.

"What . . . ? What have I done?" Xolo gasps. He claws his hair, and, unable to hold back the sobs, he lets out a deathlike cry that echoes throughout the Tower of Ice.

Out by the coastline, the death shrill startles Esteban and the oxen with fright.

CHAPTER 7
THE FOOL ARISES

April 13, 2222, 12:45 p.m.

Xolo swaddles Savani and Santa Ana's dismemberments under a discarded tent cloth he found at the razed campsite. He moistens their cadavers—the Shark Monster's leftover scraps—with the kerosine can down to the last drop. The *tecpatl* then scrapes against a small stone, and the issuing sparks set the funerary pyre ablaze. Xolo steps away from the swelling black smoke and takes a silent vigil while the ravenous flames grate his old partners down to ash.

Esteban stands beside him. The coachman is rather obtuse. He dangles his tongue out, trying to pluck one or two falling snowflakes.

"It's snow, plain old snow." Esteban suckles his lips. He smiles, content with the snow's flavorlessness. "Taste no different from the snow of yesteryear winters. You did it. You killed that thing. The curse is over, and the snow is pure again like the whiteness of Heaven."

"Nothing is pure, and nothing ever ends," Xolo retorts.

His thoughts drifted away from the snow behind a shallow glower. When the Shark Monster's dark gift marauded his soul, Xolo too, dug deep into the creature's tenebrous core, though he only managed to unbury a few truths about the creature.

Never has he encountered a foe like the Shark Monster, a foul creature whose true name is Xook, and whose dark advent and lifeblood are inextricable from the miracle of creation. The Shark Monster belongs to an ancient, preternatural tribe that bears a bitter grudge against mankind, a grudge that out-stretches back to untold millennia. Salvatore's ambition was ignorant to the dark magicks that were unearthed from the Tower of Ice— 'twas a Death God itself!

And the Shark Monster is but one of unknown incarnations still slumbering out there in the great unknown of the universe.

His hands tremble at recalling the Shark Monster's violation over his mind. There had been but one other individual who has raped him in such an unforgivable manner.

Xolo lets off a shaky sigh. He kneels to lift the third swaddled form—Santiago's desecrated corpse. Before carrying the boy's lifeless body out of the tower, Xolo made sure to stitch the arm back in place and suture the other gaping wounds. The contrite task was torturous for him, and Santiago's milky, empty eyes will deny him further sleep. He lays Santiago on the back of the carriage. Agony swells in his eyes, tears overflowing. Xolo wipes them away, praying Esteban did not take notice.

The coachman, Esteban, has no idea whose body Xolo brought back from the tower aside from the other two slain bounty killers. He does not care enough to ask, preferring the freedom of discretion and comfort of ignorance. Both hop onto the driver's box and Esteban turns to look at the simmering funeral pyre one final time.

"Were they, uh, were they friends of yours?" The coachman asks.

"No." Xolo replies with a cold breath.

"Then why bother with the fire?" Esteban asks. "Should've left their bodies back in the cave, tower, or whatever, you know, for the maggots. What little remained, anyway. I mean no disrespect. You just don't strike me like the compassionate type."

"I'm not . . ." Xolo pauses. He turns a downcast glance back to Santiago's tiny shape. "But it was the right thing to do."

"Hiya!" Esteban whips at the lead line. The oxen bellow, and they begin the long tug up through the mountains and back to Berumbo.

The carriage swerves toward the cemetery. Xolo turns his glance away from Santiago's body and back to the tower's entrance. The cold howl of Death has fallen silent and the sun's rays spear through the clouds. Off in the untouchable blue horizon, he notices a flock of seagulls returning to the western coastline. The Shark Monster has been slain, and Berumbo will soon celebrate its salvation.

But Xolo knows, though he shouldered the necessary sin—the spillage of innocent blood— the townsfolk will revile him nonetheless, and his endless track to redemption will continue with heavier footfalls.

The trotting carriage penetrates Berumbo's archway under a welcoming birdsong. Xolo whips his head around to find the secluded little bird, but instead meets the flummoxed glances of the surviving townsfolk. A small throng of five or seven families scurry out from their homes to the cobblestone road, eager to bask anew under the sun's uninhibited warmth. But their joy draws cold when they notice Xolo riding with Esteban. Xolo turns away from their glowers that mirror Osvaldo's hate and repulsion. He is more than a foreigner to their lands, but a mutant.

Bigoted fools. They've no idea that it was he, a mutant, who delivered them from perdition.

Esteban tugs the lead line closer to his chest and the oxen bellow to a rough halt. They have arrived at El Sapo's Inn's front steps. Xolo leaps off the carriage and marches down the cobble-stone walkway with the boy's stiff body cradled in his arms. He never bids Esteban farewell.

Xolo kicks in the doors, jolting Salvatore and Osvaldo off their bums. The conspiring men exchange concerned sidelong glances. Xolo walks past them, his mad glower daggering them both with stern, unforgiving contempt.

Xolo lays down Santiago's small body on the lobby couch. He is careful not to bruise it. "We have to talk . . . alone," he addresses Salvatore.

"Who do you think you are, freak? You're in no position to make such a request. There's no way in hell I'll leave you alone with him." Osvaldo snaps back. His eyes dart all round Xolo. "And where are the other two? Huh. Offed them, did you? Ah, I figured. You—*perversions*—have no honor, and you just so happen to be the worst of that unholy race. Our curse isn't over, not yet. Not until you leave this place for good, freak. Don't you think for a second that we fear—"

"Confounded Oz! Just shut up already!" Salvatore screams. His eyes never leave Santiago's mummified body. He turns to Xolo with a blank stare. "We'll talk in the conference room. Just you and I . . . you've done more than enough to earn the agreed bounty. Oz . . . please take care of this for me until I've concluded with our business. And please, be gentle." He nods to Osvaldo.

Osvaldo takes a deep breath and waits for Xolo to break down the *macuahuitl* to the sliver of obsidian. The green, prismatic blades retract from Osvaldo's Adam's apple, and he slouches over to exhale. Salvatore's intervention spared Osvaldo from his own stupidity.

Xolo tucks the sliver of obsidian back into its strap around his right thigh. He scoffs at the panting Osvaldo before following Salvatore to the conference room.

Salvatore and Xolo swerve around the check-in counter, failing to acknowledge the watchful Paciencia. She twists her lips, confused by the goings-on between her husband, Salvatore, and the mutant.

"Bless the chirping birds, hon. I wager the creature is slain." She searches the hallway corners for Savani and Santa Ana. "Where are the other two murderous numbskulls?"—she asks Xolo.

"Dead." Xolo answers back, swerving past her.

"Well, ain't that a darn shame?" Paciencia said in a tepid tone. She storms after Xolo and Salvatore. "Pity, too. I got no crocodile tears to waste on those two sons of whores. Then again, they too knew how *la danza de los diablos* would always end. Job well done, hon. You've saved our little town. Glad to see you made it out alive, at least. Say, what's going on with you two boys?" she asks, noticing their tight-lipped silence.

The conference room doors shut in front of Paciencia's confused face. Salvatore and Xolo are now alone.

Salvatore walks to the armoire with jangling keys in hand, avoiding Xolo's contemptuous glower.

"I suppose it's best we dispense with the agreed payment first." Salvatore inserts the key into the keyhole. He pauses with a shaky hand. Xolo's cold glower runs down his spine like an icepick. He swallows down his fear and turns the key to unlock the armoire. "Might I ask the need for this private audience with me? The bounty is over, and we have no further business to—"

Xolo slams something on the table. He slides it over to Salvatore without uttering a single word.

Salvatore plays possum to the leather-bound journal on the table. He considers it for a minute before reaching for it with dancing fingers. The journal had been lost to him for months now, on that accursed night when the Shark Monster was awakened from its condemned slumber. Salvatore springs it open and finds the photograph tucked between the pages. He lets off a shaky sigh and runs a yearning finger over the smiling face of his deceased son, Santiago.

"I–I don't understand. Where did—" Salvatore's breathing tightens to a sharp pant.

A spectral hand nooses a grip around his neck. The conference room quakes underneath a vengeful telekinetic push.

Xolo outstretches an open palm and lifts Salvatore off his feet before pinning him against the wall. He curls the open palm to a claw, tightening the spectral grasp around Salvatore's neck.

"Wh–What . . . are you . . . d–d–d . . ." Salvatore coughs.

"You knew, didn't you? You knew that thing was your son all along." Xolo growls with unabated anger. Salvatore nods, and Xolo twists the spectral grip harder. "He was your son— you spineless bastard! Yet you sent us in there to murder him all the same! He was your son! You should've tried saving him! You should've protected him!"

Xolo's nostrils begin to drip with blood. He loosens Salvatore from the spectral grip and lets him fall to the floor. Xolo cleans off the red strings from his nose and waits for Salvatore to catch a second wind.

"Foo . . . foo–foo—fool. He was already dead. The—the glyphs. We studied them for countless nights. They did not lie. Once that creature you so effectively slew took possession through the mask, the bond was nigh absolute . . . it made a slave out of my boy's soul. A blood sacrifice—his blood and sacrifice—was the sole means to his salvation."

Xolo shoots the wheezing man a look of abject disgust. "Then you should've sunk your own hands in his blood."

"I—I couldn't do it. I couldn't kill my own baby boy." Salvatore sobs. "No matter my cowardice, my boy received a father's mercy. And by what right do you judge me, freak! What does a bounty killer know of mercy anyway? What can *El Bastardo de Génesis* possibly understand about penance? That's right, I know who you are, what you are. And from what Oz hears, Genesis' *Infanta Reina* is demanding your head on a pike. You're no simple criminal. You're an outcast even among the other perversions of Genesis, and you're stranded in a world that hates you. You . . . you're all alone."

"If it were only that simple." Xolo said

under his breath. "You know who I am, then why am I still here?"

"Because we needed you." Salvatore growls. "You were an invaluable tool, a weapon, a means to an end."

"I'm a nobody, and I'm nobody's weapon." Xolo answers back. He then turns away to leave.

"Wait." Salvatore calls back. "What of your bounty? The guild's mandates are clear and strict. I—we can't keep it to ourselves. The guild will never allow it."

"This was never about the bounty for me." Xolo said. "But it's mine either way, isn't it? Therefore, it's in me to do as I wish with it . . . Keep it little man and rebuild your little world."

Xolo swings the doors open and Rubí's broad eyes stun him still. She heard everything, but neither she nor he shares a word with the other. The mutant storms off, away from the girl, away from the inn, never to return to Berumbo.

"Thank you." Rubí whispers, certain he will never hear her tiny voice.

Though she would like to do so much more than thank him. Rubí would like to quieten his roaring guilt and confess the truth to him—her silence is what doomed her brother, Santiago.

September 10, 2221, 11:55 p.m., the night of the massacre.

Sleep eludes Rubí. She rolls around in her sleeping bag, Salvatore's journal snuggled around her arms. Her eyes spring open to a snoring Santiago. The boy's arms still cradle the horrid basalt stone mask, and yet, the object of her earlier torture attracts her curiosity. Rubí crawls over to Santiago, and she slides the mask free from his sleeping embosom. She runs a finger around the mask's dull countenance.

"Ouch!" she cries after pricking her finger over a sharp edge.

She suckles on the blood-dripping finger. Rubí then notices an odd, soft glint bleeding from the mask's brow region. She peels away the dry mud caked over it and discovers a red stone underneath. The stone is wedged tight on the basalt stone mask and no matter how hard she tugs, Rubí cannot dislodge it.

Rubí exhales heavy with disappointment. She reaches for her father's journal, and riffles through the pages until she finds a blank one and pencils a rough sketch of the mask. Rubí curls her lips, eyes dancing between the swelling dot of blood on her finger and the pencil sketch. She breaks free from the short ceremony and smears the red stone on the sketch with her own blood. A great sense of pride surges throughout her body. This is her first archaeological discovery. Sleep finally sways her into her dreams. Rubí shuts the journal and sets it aside with the basalt stone mask laid atop it. Her weary eyes follow suit, and she falls asleep with a big smile across her face.

"Sissy. Sissy, wake up." Santiago calls out to her.

Rubí groans but submits to Santiago's pestering. Her eyes struggle through the haze of sleep, and she is confronted by the stone mask's rigid, empty glower.

"Boo!" Santiago yells out. Rubí yelps and he falls back in laughter.

"Sonny, you jerk. You—you scared me half to death." Rubí chastises. "You take that ugly thing off this instant or I'm telling father."

"No! Please don't say anything sissy. I was just having some fun. Honest." Santiago pleads. He tugs at the mask with great strain. "Hey, the mask, it–it's not coming off. It's stuck or something. Sissy . . . I–I can't breathe . . . sissy . . . help me!" Santiago cries with palpable fear.

"Sonny?" Rubí mouths in confusion, and

watches Death reawaken from its condemned slumber.

The mask's stone essence crawls round Santiago's head, devouring the boy's tiny body. Santiago's body then contorts and outstretches into a tall and lithe form; his corneas then flush with blood and his nose scrunches flat into two flaring slits. Muscles tear and bones splinter until Santiago transmutes into a grotesque creature of ashen skin that flakes like grating stone. And his pained screams, they recede into a rattling cackle.

The Shark Monster is born!

Its molten-blooded eyes shiver with reborn savagery and its third eye, perched above the brow, twirls with hungry madness. The Shark Monster presses an ebony claw up against its split lips, commanding Rubí to remain shush.

She obeys.

The Shark Monster never lays a claw on her and swims away into the shadows. Perhaps Santiago's influence shields her from its bloodlust. She will never know for certain, and the massacre unfurls without a forewarning scream.

"Daddy, that thing, it's Sonny. It took Sonny away first," she whispers to her father amid their escape from the massacre.

April 13, 2222, 4:12 p.m.

Xolo is on the train back to guild headquarters. He has just rounded off the recent bounty's report to Neza, guild master of the Bounty Killers Guild.

"So, Savani and Santa Ana are both dead." Guild Master Neza speaks from the audio-transceiver box. "Well, ain't that a fucking shame. There goes our one-month clean streak. Oz said that thing was a monster or something uglier. I ain't much for spook stories, but after everything we've experienced ... monster sounds mighty sane to me. What exactly was it, kid?'

"I–I don't know ..." Xolo stands over a steaming sink. He washes his wounds clean of blood.

"Neither of them had beneficiaries, and the guild rules are clear. The loot is all yours, kid." Neza's voice drones. "Listen, I know we've rowed about this to death already, but this purgatorial tract you've undertaken is suicidal, if not stupid. Take the loot, kid, and become a nowhere man. Obscurity is the best sort of peace men like us can ever afford."

"You're poor at subtlety, Neza. What are you trying to tell me here?" Xolo asks with a weighty tone. "I'm . . . uncomfortable with any type of doublespeak. You know this."

Neza lets off a hesitant groan. "Clara . . . she's breached a truce with Vargas, an amicable truce. Their feud is squashed, and there's no one left to dispute her right to succession. Clara's rule is now absolute. She is Genesis' undisputed *Infanta Reina*. Her wrath is impatient, too. She's already petitioned for assistance in your arrest with the World Court. You understand what this means? They're finally coming for you, the whole goddamn world. I, um, I won't be able to keep you safe for much longer, kid. I . . . I'm sorry."

Neza pauses for Xolo to say something, anything. The mutant says nothing.

Neza continues. "Take your loot and disappear. I'll knock 'em off your scent for as long as I can, okay? You hear me, kid?"

"I didn't take the loot." Xolo answers back. "It was never about the bounty for me."

"Well, can't say I'm surprised. Honor will be the death of you, kid." Neza argues. "There won't be anywhere left for you to run. But you can stop the ensuing bloodshed now if you'd just open your goddamn mouth."

"I don't care. Let them come." Xolo replies.

"I'm tired of running. Tired of playing the fool. I've no choice left except to fight."

"Just get back to HQ. We'll figure out our next move. In the meantime, don't do anything stupid 'til then." Neza disconnects in a burp of static.

The lithesome steam fogs up the mirror. Xolo continues to wash his wounds clean of blood. His glance shifts upwards to the mirror, and he attempts to pierce through the fog with narrowed eyes. He lays an open palm over the mirror and stands monolithic for some seconds.

Then . . . Isabella's distant voice pulls him back to a time long forgotten.

"One day . . . you shall make your own mark upon the world as I have. Your legacy shall be greater than my own, transcending the greater annals of history and you'll own the greatest tales ever told. I may rule under a hallowed crown, but I am but a humble servant, destined to burden a great many sins. But you, one day you will arise a true hero. Never forget this, my brave warrior . . ."

Xolo fans his flattened palm across the mirror. The streaks shave a sinister reflection of the Shark Monster. It taunts him with an ugly, crocked grin and its molten-blooded eyes sear through his damned soul. Xolo's fist shatters the reflection in a silent scream. The Shark Monster disappears, and a thin string of blood trickles down his shattered reflection beside a single tear.